She shook her head. "I can't risk it."

"What?"

"Anything more than a personal relationship with you." She shook her head again. "I mean professional."

He grinned, pleased she was flustered. "You were right the first time."

"No, I wasn't. I can help you, but not if you're going to play games."

His grin fell. "I'm not playing games."

"What happens if you're disappointed?"

He frowned. "What are you talking about?"

"What if I let you kiss me right now and it's awful?"

"It won't be."

"Will you stop working with me?" she continued. "Or will that satisfy your curiosity enough to let you realize that—"

Jason didn't hear the rest of her words. Only one important thing echoed in his mind. "You're going to let me kiss you?"

Abby threw up her hands. "Were you listening to a word I said? I said there are con—"

She didn't get to finish before his mouth covered hers. Abby felt herself sinking into sweet ecstasy as his mouth claimed hers and he crushed her body to him. His demanding lips caressed hers, his large hands exploring the hollows of her back. She now knew—not just imagined— what he felt like. He fumbled behind her, opened the door to an empty room and pulled her inside.

Books by Dara Girard

Harlequin Kimani Romance

Sparks
The Glass Slipper Project
Taming Mariella
Power Play
A Gentleman's Offer
Body Chemistry
Round the Clock
Words of Seduction
Pages of Passion
Beneath the Covers
All I Want Is You
Secret Paradise
A Reluctant Hero
Perfect Match
Snowed in with the Doctor
Engaging Brooke
Her Tender Touch

DARA GIRARD

fell in love with storytelling at an early age. Her romance writing career happened by chance when she discovered the power of a happy ending. She is an award-winning author whose novels are known for their sense of humor, interesting plot twists and witty dialogue. When she's not writing, she enjoys spring mornings and autumn afternoons, French pastries, dancing to the latest hits and long drives.

Dara loves to hear from her readers. You can reach her at contactdara@daragirard.com or P.O Box 10345, Silver Spring, MD 20914.

Her Tender Touch

Tender

Touch

DARA GIRARD

HARLEQUIN® KIMANI™ ROMANCE

To my rock (you know who you are) and my support. Thanks!

Recycling programs
for this product may
not exist in your area.

ISBN-13: 978-0-373-86382-2

Her Tender Touch

Copyright © 2014 by Sade Odubiyi

H HARLEQUIN®

Printed in U.S.A.

™ www.Harlequin.com

Dear Reader,

"I saw a woman in a kimono and she was completely naked underneath. When she bent over, it was just wrong...."

I heard this comment in a news clip featuring an etiquette coach and knew what career I wanted for Abby Baylor. A career rife with story potential got me thinking: What if a corporate etiquette coach is hired by a man with a traumatic past and a terrible temper? Enter Jason Ward.

However, Jason isn't the only one with a lesson to learn. For all his ruthlessness and rude ways, he had a tender side I didn't expect. And Abby had a harder edge that surprised me.

Fortunately, in spite of their ups and downs, the holiday season adds a nice touch to their roller-coaster romance.

Enjoy,

Dara Girard

Chapter 1

Her hands were going where they didn't belong, but they'd been doing that all evening. Jason Ward did his best to move away, but if he moved any farther, he'd fall out of his seat.

"I love a man who knows what he wants," Stephanie Armstrong said, as she purred loudly. She reminded him of a hungry feline ready for mating season. She was an attractive older woman whose husband was a possible key investor. Jason's partner, Dennis Collins, had put him in charge of keeping her entertained for the evening, but she only had one thing on her mind. And this wasn't the first time. He didn't know why the wives seemed to be drawn to him. Dennis laughed and said that, along with his good looks, he had a raw, hungry ambition their husbands lacked that sparked their interest. For a brief moment Jason thought of how he'd had to kiss up to many of them over the years, when he'd been younger and just starting out. He didn't mind the perks that came with getting a lucrative business deal, but right now he wasn't in the mood. He seized her wrist as it came too close to his manhood. His eyes met hers, and he saw them light up.

"I can make sure my husband gives you everything you want." She bent forward, giving him a clear view of her ample cleavage.

He shoved her hand away. "I'm not that desperate. Excuse me." Jason began to push his chair away. She extended her jeweled hand and placed it firmly on his forearm.

"You don't want to make me unhappy," she said in a low warning voice.

Jason took a napkin that was lying nearby and scribbled down a number, then handed it to her.

She grinned. "That's more like it."

He stood and left. Dennis saw him heading for the door and walked over to him. "Did I just see you give your phone number to that Armstrong woman?"

"No. I gave her a number, but it wasn't mine. It's for an escort service."

"Does she know that?"

"She'll find out when she calls them."

Dennis swore. "Couldn't you just flirt with her a little bit? I'm the brains and you're the—"

"The what? The stud?"

"No, I'm just saying that you need to be a little more suave in your approach to people like that…"

"Who treat me like a boy toy or some kind of sex slave they've purchased for their private use?"

"She's an attractive woman."

"Just like all the others," Jason said, bored. "You know my policy. I don't sleep with wives."

"No one is asking you to sleep with her."

"You weren't at the table—her hands were saying a lot."

"We need this deal."

Jason knew that. He and Dennis, his best friend, were

partners in a software development firm they had created several years earlier. Due to major cost overruns they had incurred developing innovative cyber-security software they had recently launched, they had discovered that their chief financial officer had been embezzling some of the funds. He had hired his girlfriend as his bookkeeper—only at the time he didn't let anyone know she was his girlfriend—who had fixed the books. Now the company was facing bankruptcy, but he and Dennis were the only ones who knew. To rectify what had happened, they had invited several key investors and speculators to a "wine-and-dine" weekend at a fancy golf retreat that cost them a fortune; but they were willing to spare no expense to get back on track. They had dismissed the CFO but desperately wanted to keep any knowledge of what had happened a secret, and had agreed not to file any criminal charges as long as he signed a nondisclosure agreement.

But somehow a rumor was spreading that the company was facing financial difficulty, and the two of them had decided they needed to make sure the investors were not nervous and felt secure with the direction the company was going. In order to avoid bankruptcy, Jason had recently forged a high-risk venture, which he hadn't revealed to the board of directors yet, with hopes it would come through in time.

Jason looked around him and swore. What was he doing? He was tired of "entertaining" wives and significant others, just to get a couple of bucks. He never wanted to be like his investors. They wore their fine tailored suits along with their weak ethics and kissed up to him when it suited them, but he knew they'd drop him in an instant. It was all just business. He knew he was in a shark-infested ocean and needed to make sure to keep his teeth sharpened.

"You know, man, you make people nervous," Dennis said.

"Are you still referring to Mrs. Armstrong?"

"No. I mean, people in general."

Jason shrugged. "So what?"

"One day, someone may want to teach you a lesson."

Jason tugged on the cuff of his jacket. "I'm already well schooled."

"The company is in trouble. Bankruptcy is not something to toy around with."

"I know why we're here. Remember, I helped build this company with you, and I won't see it fail." He walked away.

Dennis watched him go and sighed. He was wrong. He wasn't just the brains—Jason was, too, but no one would know it by the way he acted. He had the body of a wrestler and the brash manners of a street fighter. It wasn't just his intimidating build that put people on edge; he had a certain disdain—especially for individuals he could tell were only after the bottom line, no matter the cost—which he didn't mind showing. His eyes cut through them. What had once been an asset, his ability to fearlessly face whatever problem they had, was now a liability to the growth of the company. And Dennis knew the board was thinking of removing him.

"The man's a damn gorilla," one stockholder said. He could get away with saying such things in public since he was one of the biggest shareholders.

"He's jeopardizing the image of the company."

"He's also made this company rich," another said, one of the few who still believed in Jason. "He's the reason SENTEL, Incorporated is in existence."

"And he'll be the reason it fails if we're not careful."

Dennis looked over and saw Jason arguing with Mr.

Hansen, one of the key members of the board of directors. He gripped his hand into a fist and then released it. He wanted the company for himself. It was time. He no longer wanted to be overshadowed by Jason's brilliance or crass behavior. They'd risen higher than they'd both imagined, but Dennis felt that Jason was now a risk to that dream. Dennis hadn't grown up on the streets of Baltimore the way Jason had, but he'd tolerated Jason's rough ways because he made him money.

Now his usefulness was coming to an end. With the release of the new software, and the profits that would follow, Dennis felt ready to rule on his own. But he wished Gwen Duggin were here. She was the one person who knew Jason. How he thought, and why he acted the way he did. After her death, Jason had buried himself in work and buried the man he used to be. Dennis had little interest in resurrecting that man. He just wanted to find a way to remove his old friend so that he could be free of him forever.

Stephanie approached him. "You said he was a sure thing." Annoyance and hurt were clear in her voice.

"I was wrong," Dennis said, guessing from her tone that she had called the number Jason had given her.

"I don't like being made a fool of." She moved in closer to him, and he could smell the wine on her breath.

"Neither do I."

She arched a perfectly trimmed brow. "So we have a common enemy?"

"It looks that way." Dennis took a sip of his wine. "I want him gone and you want him punished, but there's not much we can do. I don't want the company to suffer."

"The company doesn't have to. I think I know a way."

"I'm listening."

"It could be risky, and he might not fall for it."

"He trusts me, and that's all you need to know."

"Good, then I know of a plan that will get him put out of the way for a long time."

As he listened to Stephanie's scheme, Dennis's smile widened.

One year later

A cold March wind blew past like a desolate breath as Jason stared at a man he'd once considered a friend. The two stood in the parking lot outside their office after a long day. "What do you mean I'm out?"

"The board voted, and we're replacing you."

"But I built this company."

"And we thank you for it. But you're a liability now."

"I can fight this. It will be a cold day in hell before I—"

"You're lucky this is all that's happening. Mrs. Armstrong accused you of assaulting her."

"What? You know I didn't touch her."

"It's her word against yours. Who do you think they'll believe? That's the problem with you, Jason. You think it's all about honesty and integrity, but in business it's about image and getting people to believe you. You know how to make money, but not everyone respects you."

Before he could reply, Jason saw them. Several men, looking very serious, wearing what looked like identical dark suits, came up to him. "Mr. Jason Ward, you're under arrest for fraud."

"What?" He stared at them, unable to process what was happening.

"I'll get you a good lawyer," Dennis said as the officers led him away.

But no lawyer could help. Dennis had skillfully turned everything Jason had done over the past year to save the company into "questionable dealings," including the high-risk venture he had discussed with Dennis *and* the company lawyers, to see if the idea, though risky, was viable. They had concurred that, although the approach appeared a little shady, he was on the *right side* of the law. Now he'd been charged with an obscure fraud violation he never knew even existed. In an instant, his image was shattered, and he knew that, although he couldn't prove it, he was being prosecuted because of jealously and false accusation, and that Dennis and Mrs. Stephanie Armstrong were behind it.

Initially, he fought the charges long and hard, but soon discovered how difficult it was dealing with the federal government. The evidence presented was stacked up against him, and without the company's wealth to back him, his lawyer told him that he wouldn't be able to win and that he should make a deal. He did and was convicted, in spite of his willingness to work with the government and the fact that he had no prior record, and was sentenced to fourteen months in a federal penitentiary.

The fall of Caesar. The last person he'd trusted had betrayed him. But betrayal and disappointment were nothing new to him. He had gone through a lot growing up in the foster care system in Baltimore. His adoptive mom had given him a chance, once he'd aged out of the system. He had no memory of his real parents. As a child he just remembered going from one home to the next and having to take care of himself.

His adoptive mom, Beatrice Ward, had made a difference in his life. She saw what others didn't. At eighteen, he'd given up on having a real family of his own; then she'd come along. He remembered now that she never liked his best friend, Dennis, when he'd introduced him to her. Dennis's parents had briefly fostered Jason, and they'd struck up a lifetime friendship. At least that's what he thought.

After graduating from high school, he'd earned a degree in industrial engineering while Dennis got an MBA, and the two friends decided to build a company together. Work had been his saving grace after Gwen died.

He still couldn't stand being alone or quiet with his thoughts, but prison had forced him to face himself. To face the harsh description of the man the prosecuting attorney had portrayed in court, saying he was a brute, ruthless, a reckless man. He would lay down his sword. There was nothing more to fight for. Everything that had mattered to him had been taken away. He couldn't even face his mother and refused to see her when she came to visit. He wanted to disappear. That was until he heard she was ill, and he knew he had to be there for her. That's when the old fire in him returned. He became a model prisoner, and with the help of a new attorney, he served only nine of the fourteen-month sentence.

Eventually the ruling was overturned, but the damage had been done. The nine months he spent being locked up had been like living in a nightmare, and he just wanted to get on with his life. While the TV cameras and news reporters had been there when he'd entered the prison, no one was there when he came out. Only a small news article was placed on the last page of the major local newspaper. He was still a wealthy man, at least on paper, but he had enormous legal fees, and his reputation was now in ruins.

Jason spent the next six months making sure his mother, who had been diagnosed with a slow-growing uterine cancer, got the care she needed. She was the most important person in his life, and although he hadn't allowed her to see him while he was in prison, she had kept sending a steady stream of note cards, one a week, which he had saved and dutifully secured in his home safe, taking time to read them every now and then.

During some of those long hours alone in his cell, he'd remembered all of her sacrifices. How much she gave up, so that he could have the life he now led.

He spent hours taking her to and from her chemotherapy appointments and hired a private-duty nurse to stay with her when he couldn't, to help her during her recovery period. After she finished the series of grueling treatments, they got the good news they both hoped for: her cancer was officially in remission. Jason then focused on rebuilding his life.

He decided to go into a business that was totally opposite of what he had done before, that wouldn't care much about his past history. He purchased a chain of time-share resorts that was in foreclosure. He would rise again and prove that he was a man of integrity. To get the business off the ground, Jason needed a partner or at least one or two investors, but no one would partner with him. He tried to convince himself that he didn't need them, he'd be fine on his own, but he knew that wasn't true. He needed partners and millions of dollars if this new venture was to succeed.

Red velvet. Abby's mouth watered, but it wasn't the cake on her plate that made her drool, or the hot August sun— it was the man she saw stepping out of a silver Lexus. He was tall, and cool like a glass of ice-cold water, the sun seeking him with its rays. He pushed up his sunglasses. She hadn't had such a visceral reaction to a man since her divorce. Maybe the reason why he'd claimed her interest was because this man seemed the complete opposite of her ex, who always worried about what others thought of him. She could tell by the way this man held himself that he didn't care who looked at him, and plenty of people did. He had a cool, disinterested air, and was dressed casually in a form-fitted sweater and jeans. He looked like a

man of finesse. Tempting, massive and beautiful. The kind
of man who could inspire poetry. Abby sighed. He was
probably taken and just a fantasy for her. For a brief moment, she imagined herself sitting at a fancy dining table
opposite him, holding up a fork with succulent oysters to
his full, beautiful lips, the steam from a cup of hot chocolate sitting between them pushing back a cold winter day.

Abby saw him enter the restaurant and sit down at a
table. She cupped her chin in her hand, watching his every
move. Then he pulled out and answered his cell phone, and
she saw his face change. It wasn't a pretty expression. It
was scary. His voice was low—a rumbling murmur, but
she heard every word. He used a string of swear words.
Her fantasy of him quickly disappeared. She'd never heard
a man be so foul. He'd be better to never open his mouth
again, she thought. Abby quickly finished her dessert, paid
the bill, then left. So much for her fantasy man.

Jason Ward was in a rage. He'd just received a phone
call from a builder at one of the resort sites where renova-
tions were being done. He'd called to let Jason know that
a worker had been seriously injured because of a foolish
oversight. Jason hated incompetence, and the fact that a
man's family would have to suffer as a consequence of a
stupid supervisor made his blood boil. If he could do everything himself, he would, but he needed to work with
others. He would have the supervisor removed.

He was finishing his rant when his mother entered the
restaurant, walked up to his table, snatched the phone out
of his hand and closed it. She was in town visiting, enjoying one of her favorite pastimes, shopping, and spending time with a close gentleman friend of hers who lived
nearby. Whenever she came into town, she stayed in an
exclusive one-bedroom condo Jason had bought for her

several years ago. It was conveniently located close to everything, including the hospital when she needed it, and she could easily use the underground metro rail to go places. This morning, the two of them had planned to meet for lunch.

Jason stared up at her, surprised. "I wasn't done yet."

"You've got to stop doing that." Beatrice pulled out a chair and sat down.

"My business?"

"Cursing. People are looking at you."

"I don't care. Do you know—"

"I don't care. This is why no one will work with you."

"I don't need anyone. See what happened last time?"

"You can't do this new venture on your own, and you know it. And bullying people won't help you either. You need to develop a new reputation if you want to rebuild your business. How can you hire the best when they don't want to work with you?"

Jason sighed. "What do you expect me to do?"

"I'm glad you asked. A friend of mine told me about this." She pushed a colorful brochure in his direction. While Jason looked the brochure over, Beatrice Ward placed her usual order, soup and salad. It was a tradition of theirs to have a mother-son luncheon when his schedule allowed. She always enjoyed the time they were able to spend together.

"What is it?" Jason asked, frowning.

"It's a flyer for an image consultant. If you want to remake your business, you need to remake your image."

"I don't have the time."

"It won't take long, and do you really want to get more phone calls like the one you just had? If you want your business to grow in the direction you want, you need to learn some business etiquette. Your temper, especially your swearing, and your lack of tact will—"

"What do you expect me to do? Handle an incompetent supervisor with kid gloves?"

"No, but first you'll learn not to interrupt someone when they're speaking."

"Okay," he agreed.

"And what if you make an employee so angry he tries to do something to your property?"

"You mean like set it on fire?" Jason laughed. He loved his mother, but sometimes she worried too much.

"Yes. You never know what someone will do when they get angry."

Yes, he did. He'd never shared with his mother his suspicion that Dennis and Mrs. Armstrong were the ones behind him getting kicked out of his company and behind his imprisonment.

And he didn't plan to. He decided to just shrug, brushing the thought away.

Two weeks later, Jason was more concerned about his mom's scheduled doctor's visit. He sat in the waiting room while she got some blood work done. To keep his mind off things, Jason went to one of the vending machines and made a selection, ready for a nice sugar rush. When the candy dropped, he picked up the packet of chocolate raisins and turned, ready to head back down the hall. He stopped when he saw a little boy, about four years old, standing near the wall, crying. No one else seemed to notice him as they rushed past. Jason waited a few moments to see if someone would stop, but no one did. He silently swore. He had to be careful—he wasn't always good with kids—but he had to find out what was wrong. He walked over to the child and knelt down to his level. "Are you lost?"

The little boy put two fingers in his mouth and stared at him.

Jason repeated his question in Spanish.

The little boy continued to stare at him, but his tears dried up.

Jason repeated the question in French.

The little boy blinked and started to suck his thumb.

Jason sighed and shrugged. "Sorry, that's all I know," he said in English. "Mama? Do you know where she is? Or papa?"

He nodded.

"Oh, so you're not lost?"

He shook his head.

If he wasn't lost, where was his guardian? He was too young to be on his own. "My name is Mr. Ward. Who did you come here with?" Jason said, softening his voice even more.

"Mama."

"Okay, and where is she?"

The little boy pointed vaguely down the hall.

"Well, you should be with her. She must be worried about you. Do you want me to take you to her?"

The child shook his head.

"Why are you crying?" He almost regretted asking. It was a hospital after all; perhaps someone he cared about was sick, or worse, had died.

The child looked at the chocolate-covered raisins in Jason's hand.

"Do you want some candy?"

The child stopped crying and nodded.

"You know, you shouldn't be talking to strangers."

He nodded but kept staring at the candy.

Jason sighed. "Okay, I'll give you one, then I'm taking you back to your mom."

He poured some candy out and started to hand it to him when he felt something hard strike the side of his face. It hit him with such force he fell over, candy scattering on the ground.

"You pervert!" a woman screamed. "Get away from my son."

Jason sat up and glared at her. "I thought he was lost."

"And you thought it was a good idea to give him candy?"

Jason surged to his feet. "You shouldn't have left him alone in the first place. What's wrong with you? You think I'd sit here giving him candy if I had something else in mind? I could have snatched him in seconds."

Her eyes widened, and she picked up her son and backed away from him.

"You're completely irresponsible leaving a young child like him alone for so long."

Tears appeared in the woman's eyes. "You have no right to talk to me like that. You don't know the stress I've been under and—"

"I don't care."

A guard approached them. "Ma'am, is this man bothering you?"

"Yes, he was trying to take my son."

The guard touched Jason's arm. "Sir—"

"I wasn't doing any such thing," he said in a low growl. "The little boy was lost, and I was just giving him some candy. I was about to take him to find his mother when this crazy woman hit me over the head with her purse and accused me of trying to steal her child!"

The woman swallowed hard, having the grace to look embarrassed. "He's right. Excuse me." She hurried away with her child.

Jason sighed, then touched the side of his face where she'd struck him. His hand came back with blood. What the hell was she carrying in her purse? Damn, he should have left the kid alone. He had just been trying to help, and she thought he had other ideas. Why did people always think the worst of him?

"What happened to you?" his mother asked when she saw him in the waiting room.

"Oh, nothing. I wasn't looking where I was going and walked into a wall," Jason lied.

"It's because you're working too much, not looking where you're going. If Gwen—" She stopped.

Were here, he said silently, finishing the sentence she couldn't.

He still missed her, even though it had been over a decade, especially at times like this when he worried about his mother. Gwen had made him feel less alone. Connected to the world in some way. He thought of the dreams they'd made for the future. Dreams that wouldn't come true. He thought of her when he'd come up with the idea for the resort—he could picture her smiling and telling him how smart he was.

"She would want you to be happy," his mother said.

He wondered if that was even possible anymore. He'd stopped being happy after her death. Partly out of guilt, but mostly despair. His business had been his life, and that had been taken from him just as she had.

Beatrice handed him the brochure again. "You need this. You have to change. You can't use fear as a factor to get respect."

He didn't want anyone to think he was easy. He demanded respect. He'd worked hard for it. As a kid, he'd been the small one who'd gotten bullied in school. He was the kid whose best friend got shot during a robbery at a gas station. He was the kid who used to be terrified he'd never escape the violence around him. But he wasn't a kid anymore, and he remembered the initial look in the young mother's eyes—it wasn't respect, it was fear. He didn't want to be feared anymore.

Jason reluctantly looked over the brochure and sighed. His mother was right. He was in a totally new field, and without partners like Dennis to be his good manners, he needed to re-create himself.

Chapter 2

She was all sugar and spice and arsenic. Judith Watson was a spiny woman and the head of the personal makeover division of Finishing Touches, Inc.

"What do you mean by that?" she asked, touching her chest in dismay as she stared at Abby. The two women sat in the main sitting area that separated their offices.

"I know you've been stealing my clients," Abby said, keeping her voice measured. She knew Judith was a snake, and she'd do her best to charm the truth out of her. "I'm sure it wasn't on purpose," she said, although she knew otherwise.

"I'm so hurt. I don't know why you would think that, much less accuse me."

"Several of my friends recommended people they know, and I wondered why none of them had come to my office or made an appointment. So I decided to do some sleuthing of my own, and discovered that at least three individuals did come to the office, but, somehow they were convinced to use your services over mine." Abby knew it had been a bad idea to share the office space with Judith in the first place but had had no other choice.

At first, things had seemed perfect. The office was in a prime location, with excellent traffic and access to ample parking. As a corporate etiquette consultant, Abby knew location was critical, and for the potential clients she was seeking, they would need to be able to get to her office easily. And the price was right. The building was part of an incubation program, designed to help new entrepreneurial ventures. But Abby couldn't afford on her own the only office that was available; it was too big. The former owner of Finishing Touches, Inc.—FTI—a company that specialized in image makeovers, had a large office with a small suite off to the side, and when Abby had seen the sign to sublet the small office, she had been thrilled.

Initially the arrangement had worked. Abby had gotten on well with the former owner, an older woman who'd given her tips about the business even though they each had a different focus, and they'd networked together. Abby worked with corporate business professionals because she had helped her ex-husband create a multimillion-dollar enterprise and learned a lot working with him. She had met him directly out of high school and fallen head-over-heels in love. He'd promised her the sun and the moon, and convinced her that she didn't need to go to college; he'd make enough money to take care of her. She'd lived a Cinderella dream, and had enjoyed her charmed life. And while she'd worked long hours, she saw it as her duty as his wife to help and support him.

They had traveled the globe and met with millionaires and successful business entrepreneurs. Since her divorce five years ago, and after unsuccessfully looking for work, she decided to go into business for herself and use the skills she had developed. Her client list was growing, but not fast enough to cover her business and living expenses. Unfortunately for her, she'd signed a prenuptial she eventually regretted. If she divorced she would get no alimony, and the property was not to be shared—leaving her with just her wardrobe and the money she had in her personal account. She'd decided that this time she'd make sure she got paid for what she'd done for free in her marriage. She'd made her husband a success, and he'd repaid her by falling for his acupuncturist—and she had ended up with nothing.

Abby was determined she wouldn't be bitter. Instead, she'd get her revenge. She'd make all those CEOs, COOs, CFOs pay for the knowledge she had, to help them develop the polish and right image the business culture demanded.

But then things began to go wrong. Very wrong. Judith wormed her way into being hired by Finishing Touches, Inc., eventually convincing the older woman that she could take over the tasks the former owner no longer wanted to do.

Abby had accepted the change, although it rankled her having to see Judith every day. A year later, the older woman suddenly retired. Unlike Abby, Judith focused solely on the superficial outer aspect of a person's image, with no depth. But since she desperately needed the space, Abby didn't care how Judith did things. She'd hoped to move out within another year since her division had been doing well, until recently.

That's when she discovered that Judith had been stealing clients from her. "I'm really hurt that you would accuse me of doing these things," Judith said.

Abby flashed a cool grin. "I know since Mrs. Frazier left that you've wanted this place to yourself. So I've decided I'm going to make that happen."

"You're leaving?"

"Yes."

"But you can't do that," she said.

Abby stared at her, amazed by her passion. "Of course I can."

Judith quickly gathered herself together. "I mean, we have an agreement."

"That's coming up for renewal."

"You don't need to be hasty about this. I'm sure there's just been a misunderstanding somewhere."

My first misunderstanding was that you were a decent human being. "No."

"Abby, dear, I would hate for something small like this to break up the relationship we have. This is an excellent location and—"

"You'll do well." Abby was in no mood to listen to any more of Judith's lies. She knew she was crafty, but to deliberately steal her clients? That was a new low, even for her.

"It was an accident. I wouldn't have done that to you. You know how much I—"

"Cut it out. I hate when you do that," Abby said in a tone that let Judith know she was on to her.

"Why don't we start over? I have a couple of clients I haven't been able to get to yet due to my busy schedule."

"We have different clients. I don't do personal image makeovers. You know I strictly work with business professionals. I'll leave by the end of the year," Abby said, then left and went into her office.

Judith watched her go with growing panic. Abby couldn't leave. She couldn't afford the space by herself, but she didn't want to tell her that. Yes, she had been misleading several of Abby's clients because, for some reason, things had slowed down and she wasn't bringing in the amount of money she needed, and she had gotten desperate. She had to save face. Damn, she hadn't thought she'd catch on so quickly. After Mrs. Frazier had left, the business hadn't been doing well, and there was more interest coming to Abby. It didn't make sense. Why did anyone need corporate etiquette over personal image makeovers? Besides, she didn't see that much of a difference in what they did, and, fortunately, neither had the clients who'd come in for consultation. Since they shared the same office and computer system, it hadn't been hard to access the main data system and change schedules.

Abby always acted so superior. Judith knew she was prettier, but Abby had a striking beauty that always got a second look. Judith was irritated that although Abby couldn't afford her own office space, she acted as if she could buy the building if she wanted to. That had always annoyed her, but now she had to convince her to stay. When the phone rang she brushed her problems aside and put on her voice. "Finishing Touches, Judith Watson speaking."

"How full is your client list?" a woman asked in a brusque tone.

"I never turn away business," Judith said as pleasantly as she could.

The woman sighed. "You may want to with this one. He needs a major makeover, and might be difficult to work with."

Judith lifted her brows, intrigued. "What do you mean by that?"

"He needs help fast, but I'm not sure he's convinced yet."

"And you are?"

"His mother. He's a little rough around the edges, but he's a good man and I don't want to set him up for failure if you're not up for it."

Judith thought back to one torturous client she had dealt with. He'd caused her to lose twenty pounds over six months, and refused to pay her at the end because he did not feel that she had met his standard.

"If you're interested, he'll pay well. Money's not a factor."

Yes, she needed the money, but not at this rate. Besides, she preferred working with women more than men, and if his own mother thought he was difficult, Judith knew her time with him would probably be miserable. Why did Abby have to threaten to leave? Abby? Hmm. "Okay, is he in business, by any chance?"

"Yes, he runs his own company and has just started a new venture."

"And his name?"

"Are you interested in taking him on?"

"No, but I know someone I can refer him to. A colleague I work with here in the same office. You can rest assured that I'll be very discreet."

"His name is Jason Ward."

"One moment, please. I have another call." Judith put the woman on hold, then quickly did an online search for Jason Ward. She saw that he'd been booted from his former company several years ago and had spent time in prison. She gave a low whistle. "I'll make an appointment for tomorrow at 6:00 p.m. Will that work?"

"I'll let him know." The woman disconnected.

Judith hung up the phone and couldn't help a smile. She did a little dance in her office, then smoothed down her hair and clothes and walked over to Abby's suite.

"I don't want any hard feelings between us," Judith said, entering and taking a seat.

"'I don't have any feelings at all," Abby said, not looking up from what she was doing.

Judith fought not to grit her teeth. "I just got a new client, who I thought of referring to you, but if you're not interested…" She began to stand.

"I didn't say that."

Judith leaned back, trying not to look too satisfied. She'd gloat later. "He's very wealthy and starting a brand-new business. I know that's your area. If you think you can handle him."

"I can handle anyone."

"Don't be overconfident."

Abby narrowed her eyes. "What do you mean? I'm good at what I do."

"He may be too much for you. I hear he can be a bit of a bully."

"I can turn a tiger into a pussycat. Who is he?"

"Jason Ward."

Judith watched her with interest. She could almost see Abby's mind working and trying to place him. To her delight, she didn't. "So, why does he need you?"

"As I said, he's starting a new business, and while I can help him with his image, I thought you might be a better match, since you're into corporate business and stuff. Besides, he's offering a lot of money."

"How much?"

Judith threw out a ballpark figure, just to get Abby interested.

"That's a lot of money to pass up. And that's not like you."

"I'll take the case if you want. I'm only telling you this as a show of good faith. I really hate you thinking that I was doing something so unethical, such as stealing clients from you. I mean, we are family and—"

"Fine," Abby cut in, not wanting to talk about the tumultuous relationship she shared with her sister.

"Good, I'll give him your number, but only on one condition."

"What?"

"You'll stay. If you can change Jason Ward in six weeks, I'll cover the cost for your office suite for the next six months." Judith knew it was a gamble since she wouldn't be able to afford it, but she was already convinced Abby wouldn't succeed.

"Okay."

Judith smiled and held up a finger to indicate that she wasn't finished. "But if you don't succeed in changing him within six weeks, you'll sign for another two years." Judith knew she had baited Abby. Abby hated to pass up a challenge. "So, you'll make sure he's scandal-free and the darling of the business world by the end of six weeks?"

"You can count on it."

Abby knew the snake was up to something, but she didn't care. Jason Ward would be a coup for her. After Judith left, she looked him up on her computer and then gripped her hands into fists when his handsome face came on the screen. That Jason Ward! He would be a nightmare. The man who refused to wear suits, who only wore two colors, who cursed with a fluency that would make a sailor blush. Uncouth, uncultured and undeniably intriguing. A man who kept his private life guarded. And a man who reminded her of someone. Oh, no…the man from the restaurant!

Abby stood and kicked a chair in frustration. Outside, a late October wind brushed past her window. Judith had set her up for failure. But the fact that he was seeking help meant that he wanted a change, and in spite of herself, she was confident she could help him. Besides, a referral from him would open doors she could only imagine. Her unorthodox methods may be just what he needed. Abby could already see herself affording a new apartment and car. She wanted to regain the life she'd lost after her divorce, and Jason Ward was the key.

Chapter 3

As Jason rode the elevator, he kept asking himself why he had allowed his mother to make the appointment. She had reminded him that it was time for him to work on his professional demeanor.

"You have to get a handle on your temper," she had said to him when he'd changed his mind about the consultation. She had been trying to help him rein in his temper since the day she had adopted him. "I wish there was a man in the house to show you how to behave sometimes." Jason had resented her insinuation that he needed a man to show him how to be one. But he knew he needed help.

Sure, he could make money, but SENTEL was the second business he had lost. He remembered the recycling business he'd started with a friend during high school. It had done well, financially, but his temper and mood swings had caused them to break up. He started SENTEL, Inc. after the tragic loss of his girlfriend, Gwen, and had had that stolen from him. Although the members of the board listed his personality as a reason for his dismissal, he knew there was more. In addition to his temper, he knew he also lacked tact. But he hadn't been tactless with that Armstrong woman.

While Dennis had no objection to crossing the line with married women, that was one boundary Jason would not violate. He respected his mother too much. He enjoyed women, all sorts of women, but hated the ones who felt entitled to whatever they wanted, at whatever cost.

He had found relationships with people in general to be confusing at times, which was why, when he'd had to complete hours for community service in order to graduate from high school, he'd volunteered to work with animals. They didn't need him to be anything other than himself. When he said "sit," they understood, unlike the Mrs. Armstrongs of the world who lived by their own rules.

Jason stepped off the elevator and walked to the office directly in front of him and entered, then stopped when he saw the woman sitting there. He hoped she wasn't the one. He didn't like her smile; he didn't trust her. He'd learned early that there were few women he could—or would—trust.

"Hello," she said, stretching out her hand. "You must be Jason Ward."

"Yes," he said, seeing her wince when he shook her hand, even as her smile remained. He found it too wide; her body was too close. He could see her sizing him up—calculating the price of his clothes. She'd be disappointed. If this was Abby Baylor, he'd do the initial consultation and then find someone else.

"Would you like some coffee?" she asked, gesturing to a seat.

He sat. "No, I'm fine. Thanks, Ms. Baylor."

"Oh, no, that's not me."

Before she could explain further, the other office door opened and another woman walked out. Now, she was a vision. She was tall, brown-skinned, with shoulder-length black hair, and elegantly dressed in a fitted sheath dress that showed off all her curves. She didn't smile at him or step close. He liked her immediately.

"Jason Ward?" she asked in a curt manner.

He stood. "Yes."

She held out her hand. "I'm Abby Baylor."

He shook her hand. "A pleasure."

She winced and rubbed her hand. "Not with a handshake like that. Are you trying to break my fingers? Never mind, we'll work on that later." She turned to her office. "Please, follow me."

She didn't have to ask twice. He'd have no problem following her anywhere. He liked the view from the back of her as much as from the front.

Abby walked into her room, trying to get her heart to stop racing. She'd tried to imagine what Jason Ward would be like, but nothing had prepared her for the man she met up close. A man who was both terrifying and mesmerizing. She knew him by reputation. He made news for his ruthless dealings and temper. But strangely, he didn't frighten her, although he should have. She was struck by his dark, cutting gaze. He topped six-four, had a remarkable build and looked like a man who could carry tree trunks—or better yet, a helpless woman over his shoulder. She'd wanted a challenge, and she knew he would be one.

"We have a lot of work to do. I can already list three things we need to work on. Take a seat."

"Is this how you greet all your new clients?" he said, still standing.

"Why? Should I be a little gentler?"

He lifted a brow but didn't reply.

Score one for her, Abby thought with a small thrill

of delight. She'd put on her cool demeanor on purpose and wanted to see how he would react. To her amazement he didn't, but she wouldn't underestimate him. She could imagine his mind working on another strategy, so she had to take control first. She held out her hand. "Let's start again. It's nice to meet you. I'm Abby Baylor."

Jason shook her hand, his grip strong. "A pleasure."

She flexed her fingers. "Yes, we'll definitely have to work on that." She sat down. "Now tell me what you want, specifically."

Jason smiled at her as if she'd asked him something more intimate, making her skin grow warm. Although her insides trembled, she held his gaze. She would not let him intimidate her in spite of the fact he was suddenly making her very curious about what he wanted and if she could oblige him. *In his dreams,* she thought, quickly brushing the idea aside.

"I want to play well with others," he said in a sarcastic tone, taking a seat across from her.

"And not be the bully in the sandbox?"

"Something like that."

"May I give you a brief assessment?"

He shrugged. "You say that as if I have an option, but somehow I doubt it. Please, proceed. Tell me what's wrong with me."

Abby pointed to his hands. "The handshake is too hard." She nodded at him. "And the stare too long. You haven't blinked or moved your gaze once since I started talking. To someone else, that's an aggressive move. Is that what you're trying for?"

"I thought I was being attentive."

She smiled. "No, you don't. You don't want to be here."

Jason lifted a brow, but again, didn't respond.

"How long have you been doing this?" he asked.

"Don't ask questions you already know the answer to."

"Why would I do that?"

"I don't know, you tell me. You're a meticulous man. I don't think you'd hire someone you knew little about. My website and brochure say plenty about me, as do client testimonials, so, please, don't waste our time."

"I wanted to see if you'd lie."

"You'll have to ask me another question. Later. Right now I'm here to help you." She stood. "We'll start with your handshake."

He reluctantly stood. "I see you don't believe in chit-chat."

"Time is money."

"I have a lot to spend."

"The sooner we start, the sooner you'll succeed."

He shook his head, amused. "Do you always talk like that?"

"Like what?"

"In platitudes?"

"Doesn't matter. Now, the handshake is important..It says a lot about you. You don't want one that is too strong or too weak. You want a firm, assured, but quick connection. Let's try it again." She held out her hand. "Hello, I'm Abby Baylor."

He took her hand in his. This time his grip was not too strong; instead it was amazingly gentle but firm. "Jason Ward."

"That was great! Perfect. Now, look down at our hands. Do you see how nice the grip is?" She glanced up at him. "You're not looking."

"I prefer looking at you."

Abby's heart picked up its pace, and she took a deep breath to calm herself. She couldn't afford to be attracted to him. He was a client; he couldn't be anything more. She had to stay in control. "You have a hard time when you're not the leader, don't you?"

"I don't mind you being the leader, but that doesn't mean I have to follow all your directions."

She pulled her hand away. "Yes, it does. Listening to me means that you trust me."

"I don't give away my trust easily."

"If you want me to help you, you'll have to learn fast."

"I have no trouble learning fast," he said in a low voice. "But when it comes to trust, I always take my time."

Abby swallowed, wishing her heart would return to its normal pace. "Fine."

"I'd like to practice the handshake again." He moved in closer to her.

"You don't need to. I told you, you were perfect."

Jason flashed a wolfish grin. "I'm far from that." He held out his hand.

"Okay, one last time. This time you do the introductions."

He extended his hand. She took it.

"Hello, Ms. Baylor, I'm Jason Ward, and I look forward to working with you over the next several weeks."

She knew the words to say, but they wouldn't escape her mouth. Her throat felt dry; her face felt warm. She was in trouble. He was not only both terrifying and magnificent, he was sexy as hell. He softened his grip, making it restraining but also tender—staying on the side of decency, so she couldn't scold him, but eliciting very indecent thoughts in her mind. Unsettling her. He made her realize how large his hand was, how hot his palm felt against hers. Abby pulled her hand away and folded her arms. He was more devious than she thought. Maybe he was getting her back for her cold greeting—whatever the reason, she couldn't fight him on equal terms. He clearly had the advantage. But she couldn't let him have an emotional advantage; she had to stay distant and professional.

"That was perfect," she said in a bright voice, hoping he couldn't see his effect on her. "You really are a fast learner." She had learned that stroking a man's ego always worked in her favor. She just needed him as a client, nothing else. She took a step backward.

"I am a fast learner, but you're also a good teacher."

"Yes, and I also know when I'm being tested. That bone-crushing handshake before was a test, wasn't it? What were you trying to find out? Whether I'd run away or not? Whether you could frighten me? Did I pass?"

He folded his arms, and a slow smile spread across his face. "Yes." He shrugged. "I wanted to see how desperate you were."

"I'm not desperate." She moved to go behind her desk, but he blocked her path.

"Eager, then," he smoothly corrected.

"What do you mean by eager?"

He took out his cell phone and typed in a few things, then held the screen out to her. "Finishing Touches isn't doing as well as it used to. You were right. I am meticulous and did my homework. I know a lot about you, Ms. Baylor."

"And I obviously don't know enough about you. I knew you were a jerk, I just didn't realize how big." Abby stared at the screen in humiliation, feeling exposed and ashamed. She didn't care if he did or didn't want to be there, but she'd at least thought he respected her. "I see," she said coldly. She pushed past him and walked to the door.

"Where are you going?"

As far away from you as I can get. "I'm not going anywhere. You're the one who's leaving," she said, although she hated the thought of failing before she'd even begun. She'd been so hopeful about this meeting. She'd imagined succeeding with him and seeing her business soar—instead he'd shown her how close to the brink she was. "You've made it very clear that this won't work, and I agree with you," she said, opening the door wider, a signal for him to leave.

"I had to do it," Jason said in a flat, grim tone, walking toward her.

Abby stepped backward but found herself with nowhere to go and her back against the door.

Jason shoved his hands in his pockets. "I hate needing anyone. Especially for something like learning how to 'work with people.' I don't see why I should have to use someone like you. I'm good at what I do. I like my life, but for some reason people seem to have a problem with the way I do things. I don't like to depend on anyone. Finding your weak spot makes me feel fine about you knowing mine. You need me as much as I need you."

She didn't want it to be true, but he was right. "I demand respect," she said. "No more tests."

He held up his hand as though stating an oath. "Agreed."

"I can help you learn business etiquette." When he didn't look convinced, she continued. "I know it may sound strange, but in the corporate world, knowing the rules is what really counts, not just making money. You need to change your business approach, because you are your business. I'm going to show you how to be strong but not rude, kind but not weak and bold but not a bully."

"How?"

"You'll see." She sniffed the air. "My goodness, do you always smell this good?"

He blinked. "What?"

She leaned in closer and sniffed again. "Hmm." She leaned back and nodded. "I can already tell right away what some of your problems are. First of all, you smell amazing, but a little too much so—it's distracting. Is it cologne or aftershave? We may have to change it. Also, I know that you don't like wearing suits, but this present look—" she studied his khakis and the sweater he was wearing "—may be too casual for you. You're sexy, but your clothes work against you because you're projecting an aggressive sexiness that both attracts and repels at the same time. You have a very intimidating build and you're very smart, brilliant in fact, but you don't look it."

She held up her hand. "I'm not saying you look stupid, it's just that your mind isn't the first thing people think about when they look at you." *It certainly wasn't for me.* "Your build and your face work against you in the business environment where they no doubt worked for you on the streets. You'll need the right armor. You don't hide your feelings well either. Right now I know I said something that's made you angry. I'll find out what later, but I shouldn't know that. I'll teach you how to guard your feelings." She shoved his shoulder backward. "I'm going to remove this big chip from your shoulder and help you get the respect you want. I can see that's what you're hungry for. You want to prove yourself. That's a bad thing."

Jason lifted a brow in a silent question.

"When you want to prove something to someone else, you make that person important. By making them important, you make them matter. And if you make them matter, they own you." She walked back to her desk and sat. "We'll have three rules. One, you will learn to look away. It will be brief, but necessary. Two, you'll alter your appearance, not radically but enough, and three, you will not swear. Every time you swear, you'll give me one hundred dollars."

He swore. "A hundred?"

She held out her hand. "You can afford it."

He bit his lip, reached into his pocket and handed her a hundred dollar bill.

Abby carefully folded the bill and put it away. "Now, humility—"

"Is a trait I prefer not to fake."

"Do you really want my help?"

"No, I already told you that. I really don't want to be here. Take dogs and cats, for example. I have no problem with them. During high school I volunteered at a local veterinary clinic. I loved it. I never had to worry about hurting their feelings."

"We're not talking about cats and dogs. We're talking about you being able to interact well with human beings so that you make the kind of connections you need to have a successful business.

"You mean, learn how to engage in small talk and suck up to people to get what you want and—"

"What have you heard?"

"What do you mean?"

"You're talking in vague statements—'sucking up to people' and 'hurting people's feelings.' You don't strike me as the kind of person who cares what people think, but when it comes to business, I'm sure you know it's important. Something must have happened for you to be here. What's one opinion or something someone has said that you want to change?"

He hesitated.

"Nothing you say will leave this room, but I need to know how you're perceived so that I can help you."

"Your description of me was pretty accurate." He stretched his long legs and sank farther into the plush chair.

"Not accurate enough. What do people get wrong about you?"

Jason frowned. "I didn't come here for a counseling session."

"Are you scared to tell me?"

His gaze pierced hers. "I'm not scared."

"Are you afraid that I'll think the same?"

"I'm not afraid either."

"Then, tell me. What's stopping you? You can trust me. What are they saying about your brand?"

"My brand?"

"Yes. Say you're a car. What are people saying about it?"

"It's cheap, comes from a bad lot. It has a good engine but nothing else."

"And what do you want them to say?"

"I want to be a stellar model. You know, a BMW can break down and no one will say that it's worthless, but I'm like a…a few mistakes and I'm no good and no one expects me to be."

"Exactly, so you have to be clever. Because you don't have the background, you have to create an image that is incorruptible, so that people can come up with excuses for you so that *they'll* look good. You're an easy target right now. We'll change that."

Before ending the session, Abby gave Jason some paperwork to complete and made an appointment for him to attend the next meeting of the local Chamber of Commerce. "You are to dress in business attire, and make sure you introduce yourself to at least three people and exchange business cards. Oh, and by the way, I'll be the keynote speaker at the event. I'll see you next week."

"Isn't it customary to shake hands at the end of a meeting?" Jason asked when Abby remained seated behind her desk.

"No, and in some countries the man waits for the woman to hold out her hand first."

He held out his hand. "Fortunately, I'm not in one of those countries."

Abby sighed, stood and took his hand. He shook it, then brought it to his lips. "I'm sorry about the handshake," he said, his breath warm against her skin.

Abby swallowed, fighting to keep her tone neutral instead of breathless. "You're forgiven."

He kissed the back of her hand, then released her. "Thank you."

"You're welcome," she said, the back of her hand feeling as if it were on fire. "And don't kiss a woman's hand like that unless you want to get into trouble."

Jason only grinned, his eyes making it clear that he welcomed trouble and all its consequences.

Jason got in his car, then pumped his fist in the air. *Thank you, Mom.* Christmas had come sooner than he'd expected. He'd never imagined that the right woman for him would show up like this. She had intrigued him from the moment he laid eyes on her. Not because she was attractive, which she was, or smart, but she wasn't afraid of him. That was the biggest turn-on. She'd boldly met his gaze, as if challenging him to see how far he would go. The handshake was nothing. He'd had to restrain himself from pulling her closer so that he could inhale her perfume and feel her body against his. He wanted to see what she was like when she wasn't thinking of business. He wanted to make her think of something else. He now had a new goal.

His cell phone rang. He looked down at the number and grinned. "Right on time."

"How did it go?" Beatrice asked. "Did you scare her away?"

"She doesn't scare easily."

"That's good. So you'll give her a chance?"

I plan to give her a lot of things. "Yes. You can pat yourself on the back. You were right. She's just what I need."

Abby had prepared herself for a number of things. But fierce attraction hadn't been on her list. She'd assessed him well, but she hadn't assessed him completely. He'd constantly caught her off guard, at one moment insulting her, then complimenting her in the same breath, not giving her a chance to know which it was or how to respond. Should she be pleased or offended? He knew more about his appearance than he was letting on. She wondered if he really thought he needed her services. He obviously didn't seem to think he needed to change.

What she hated most was how he made her heart race—that he made her notice him as a man instead of as a client. She hadn't felt that way in a long time. His behavior was nothing new. She'd been hit on by clients before, but he was different. She wouldn't be able to brush him aside. She briefly glanced at her hand, still feeling the sensation of his skin against hers.

He was a lot bigger than she'd expected. Gruffer, too, but she wasn't intimidated; she could already see him transformed.

He'd surprised her with his calm manner. She'd been ready for his temper, outrage, a cool superiority. But he'd displayed none of those traits. She'd learned early on that it was best to keep her distance. Her cool demeanor kept a safe wall between herself and her clients, but Jason Ward was quickly melting it. And she couldn't let him. Abby knew she would have to push away any preconceived notions and see what he was really about if she was going to help him.

* * *

"So, what is he like?" Judith asked Abby the next day. "I was worried about you. I could hardly concentrate. How awful was he?"

Like I'd tell you. "I really shouldn't discuss clients."

"I do it all the time." There was a moment of silence. "That difficult, huh?" she said with pity.

"He's a fast learner."

"Is that supposed to mean something?"

"Exactly what I said."

"You know, if you don't feel comfortable with him, you don't have to do this. Just admit you can't do it. There are other clients."

But none like Jason Ward, Abby thought. She couldn't wait to see him again. Because he was a challenge, nothing else. She'd seen his magnetism, and she would use it to keep a distance. She'd seen where her words bothered him; when she'd mentioned that women found him attractive, his gaze had gone hard. She'd have to figure out why. She was very curious. What was the key to unlocking the man behind the armor?

"I'll be fine," she said, but she already knew that was a lie.

Chapter 4

Jason stared at his reflection in the full-length mirror. It had been a long time since he'd cared about how he looked, but Abby had changed his mind. He wasn't into wearing a double-breasted suit or matching finely crafted leather shoes. The casual merino wool slacks and pressed silk shirt and tie would have to do. He wanted to make sure he made the right impression.

Unfortunately, things didn't quite turn out the way he wanted. The Chamber of Commerce meeting was being held in one of the main office buildings downtown, and due to a major water break, traffic had to be rerouted. Although he had left with plenty of time to spare, deciding to take himself instead of using his driver, Jason found himself walking into the meeting forty-five minutes late. Abby was just finishing her presentation when he entered, and did not acknowledge him. She closed her speech and took a seat up front. Jason sat patiently through the next two presenters, then when everyone was dismissed to spend the rest of the time networking, he hastily made his way over to where Abby was sitting.

"Sorry I was late," he said. "There was a major water problem and parking was limited and…"

"That doesn't matter now. Just shake hands and be nice." She turned to leave.

"I'm sorry I missed your presentation."

"I told you it doesn't matter."

"But you're angry."

She folded her arms. "I'm disappointed. Would you have been late if you had an appointment with the president?"

"What?" Jason paused, wondering what she was up to. "If you had been the president, I hope your secret service men would have made arrangements for your guests to be escorted through the mess outside, so they wouldn't have…"

Abby glanced around the room. "All of these other people made it on time. You know why? Because they checked before they left, and added enough time, so they would make it. Isn't that right, Mr. Brant?" She turned and spoke to a slimy-looking gentleman standing just behind her.

"It sure is. I checked my phone and GPS to make sure I'd get here on time. I wasn't going to miss your presentation for nothing," he said, his eyes raking over Abby's body in a way that made Jason grit his teeth.

Look, but don't touch, Jason thought, sizing the man up just in case he had to make himself clear.

When Jason didn't reply, the other man continued. "A fine woman like her deserves to be the focus of a man's attention. Isn't that right, Abby?"

Abby laughed a little nervously, but Jason could tell she felt uncomfortable. "Mr. Brant, that's not—"

"I mean, if I could get just a few minutes alone with…"

Jason's temper snapped. That was as much as he could take. "I need to see you outside for a moment."

"Jason, it's okay."

"Now." His gaze never left the man.

Abby grabbed his arm and pulled him toward the door. "Jason, I have to talk to you."

He glared at the man, then let her lead him outside. "What?" he asked, once they were in the hall.

"Congratulations. You have just failed your first test."

"Test? I thought we weren't doing tests anymore."

"You can't, *but* I can. I'm the teacher, remember?"

He rested a hand against the wall behind her. "Yes, I remember."

"Nicholas Brant is a dear friend of mine."

"You mean what happened in there was an act?" he asked, doing his best to rein in his temper.

"Yes," Abby said in a clipped tone. "I wanted to see what you would do. How you would respond."

"How was I supposed to respond?"

"With more tact. Not so aggressive. You looked like you wanted to slug him."

"I did." He sighed, hating that he'd disappointed her when today had meant so much to him. He'd wanted to make a good impression, but he kept failing. First, missing her presentation and now, this. "I didn't like how he was treating you."

"And that's not the problem," Abby said, softening her tone, as though he were a wayward child she wanted to correct. "You could have just led me away." She smiled briefly. "However, the look you gave him was eloquent enough."

He drummed his fingers against the wall with irritation. "That sounds like something from out of a textbook, not real life. What would you have done if you were me?"

She paused. "If I were you?"

"Yes. What would you have done if you saw a beautiful woman you were attracted to being disrespected by another man?"

Abby opened her mouth to say something, then closed it and shook her head. "That's not a fair question."

"Why not?"

"Because it's hypothetical. What really happened in there was about a man who was embarrassed about being late, who was annoyed that he had to come here in the first place and who wanted to handle his frustration by throwing some punches."

Jason narrowed his gaze. "I thought you knew me better than that."

Abby licked her lips. "I do."

He watched the motion with interest, wishing he could moisten them some more for her. "Then why would you discount the fact that I'm attracted to you?"

"How you feel about me is not the issue here."

"How come?"

Abby licked her lips again. He groaned inwardly, wishing she'd stop doing that. "Do I make you nervous?"

"You make me angry."

He sighed, wanting so badly to kiss her, he had to grip his hand into a fist. "I'm sorry I missed your presentation," he said with sincerity. "I won't do that next time."

"Don't worry, there won't be a next time. Right now you need to focus on smiling and shaking hands."

He caught and held her gaze. "The only hand I want to hold is yours."

"Jason."

His gaze dropped to her lips. He wanted to do more than hold her hand. "Don't pretend you don't feel it, too." He met her eyes, seeing the sizzling awareness in her gaze that mirrored his. "From the first moment, I knew you were the one."

She shook her head. "I can't risk it."

"What?"

"Anything more than a personal relationship with you." She shook her head again. "I mean professional."

He grinned, pleased she was flustered. "You were right the first time."

"No, I wasn't. I can help you, but not if you're going to play games."

His grin fell. "I'm not playing games."

"What happens if you're disappointed?"

He frowned. "What are you talking about?"

"What if I let you kiss me right now and it's awful?"

"It won't be."

"Will you stop working with me?" she continued. "Or will that satisfy your curiosity enough to let you realize that—"

Jason didn't hear the rest of her words. Only one important thing echoed in his mind. "You're going to let me kiss you?"

Abby threw up her hands. "Were you listening to a word I said? I said there are con—"

She didn't get to finish before his mouth covered hers. Abby felt herself sinking into sweet ecstasy as his mouth claimed hers, and he crushed her body to him. His demanding lips caressed hers, his large hands exploring the hollows of her back. He was hard and hot, sending her senses reeling. In his arms she no longer felt like a cold day, but like a hot summer night. She now *knew*—not just imagined—what he felt like.

He fumbled behind her, opened the door to an empty room and pulled her inside. Jason was delicious, like double fudge chocolate, and although he could be misunderstood, she felt she knew him more than any man she'd ever met. When she heard him groan, then suck in his breath in surprise, she pulled away and noticed her hand had dipped dangerously below his belt. He was clearly aroused. She shoved him away, horrified by her behavior. "I am so sorry," she said, coming to her senses with a painful thud.

"Don't be," Jason said quickly. "It's nice to know you're as eager as I am."

He could be casual about it, but she couldn't. "No, that was wrong, and I sincerely apologize. I promise it won't happen again," she said, breathless but fighting for composure.

"You're joking, right?"

"I made a mistake."

"No, you didn't. Let me treat you to dinner."

"I can't," Abby said, sounding miserable to her own ears. "I feel awful, you're my client and I—"

"Okay, okay," Jason said quickly. "We have five more weeks. As long as I'm your client, I'll behave myself. But after that, you'll give me a chance. Agreed?"

"Yes."

He held out his hand. "Let's shake hands on it."

Abby couldn't help a smile. She rested a hand on her hip and said in a flat tone, "No."

"Kiss?" Jason asked, undeterred.

"No."

"Hug?"

She shook her head.

"Come on," Jason said, his voice dipping into a velvety tone of persuasion. "There has to be some way to seal the deal."

Abby folded her arms. "You'll behave the next five weeks?"

"Yes."

"Then okay." She held out her hand.

Jason grabbed it, pulled her to him and kissed her—it felt like both a vow and a promise.

When he pulled away, he winked. "I thought this agreement deserved a double seal," he said. "Now I'll go do my homework."

Chapter 5

She was back in control, Abby thought as she dived to the bottom of the pool. She would hold him off for five weeks. After five weeks, she would come up with a reason not to see him again. She wanted to, but she knew she couldn't. He made her forget things—like how important her business was and how dangerous a man like him could be. He made her feel reckless. Jason Ward was going to drive her insane. Abby squeezed her eyes closed and shut out the sound around her. Suddenly, she felt arms grab her, then drag her to the water's surface. She gasped, her lungs burning as oxygen filled them.

"Are you okay?" the lifeguard asked.

"I'm fine."

He released her. "You were down there so long you had me worried."

She blinked and wiped water from her eyes. "I'm sorry. I was just training myself to hold my breath longer," she lied.

"Well, be careful."

"I will."

Abby got out of the pool and grabbed her towel. Yes, Jason Ward was driving her insane. Unfortunately, she was enjoying every minute of it. She wanted to rip his clothes off, and if no one had been watching, she would have made his kiss a little naughtier. No, a lot naughtier. He read her too well. She had to be more careful. She had to be sensible. They would regret making their relationship anything more than business. But she could fantasize, and she did—often and in full color. Twice already, she'd replayed their kiss, but she had been the one who had him up against the wall.

Swimming had always helped to clear her thoughts, but now they felt more muddied than ever. Abby showered and changed, then went home where she lay on the couch and stared up at the ceiling. She wanted to forget the feel of his arms around her, and the taste of his tongue. She could throw caution to the wind and take him up on his offer, but doubted that would get her far. She hardly knew him. Okay, so she knew more than most, but just like when she'd first seen him at the restaurant, she was certain there was a lot more to him than met the eye.

That was the problem. She was attracted to him. She frowned. Charles had been a mistake, too. Men couldn't be her focus right now. Her attraction to Jason was a passing fancy, and she was just lonely. She didn't care what his intentions were. Whether he wanted her for a night or longer didn't matter; she didn't trust them. She didn't trust herself.

Had he gone crazy? Why had he given her five weeks? *Five weeks!* He could hardly last four days. Jason shook his head and ran faster, the biting cold invigorating. A gray sky hung overhead, but it was still too warm for snow. He'd run this route many times, but now the trees and the road were a blur. How could she deny the chemistry between them? He knew she felt it, too. He'd felt it when he'd held her in his arms. He could still remember the soft feel of her body against his. As he'd held her, he wanted to strip her naked and make love to her. He could imagine the softness of her skin against his, his thigh against hers, the fullness of her breasts and the warmth of her body beneath his.

Five weeks? He swore. He had to change her mind. It wouldn't be easy, but he didn't care. He wanted to explore her soft curves in bed.

With Gwen, it had been love at first sight. One look at her, and he had felt his world tilt on its axis. She'd smiled at him and melted his heart.

He sighed. Abby hadn't smiled at him. And she hadn't made his heart melt; instead she made him feel as if he were on fire. Those sharp, dark eyes of hers piercing through the wall he'd built around himself. She wasn't supposed to do that. It still shocked him that she'd won him over so completely. But since she'd already shaken his world, he was determined he wasn't going to let her go.

During the next meeting in the office, they discussed how Jason's temper got in the way of him getting to know anyone else at the Chamber of Commerce, and Abby decided on another exercise. As they were getting ready to leave, she said, "Oh, by the way, you're taking me to lunch."

Lunch had been an inspired idea. Usually she had clients take her to their office so that she could observe them mingle and interact with their staff. But Jason wasn't like any other client she had had before, and Abby wanted to handle him differently. She let him choose where they would go and half expected a fast-food restaurant, but Jason again surprised her by taking her to a soul food place called Southern Taste that was small, cozy and authentic.

She didn't get the feeling of pretense. She saw pride in the establishment from the delicate touches of the small crystal vases and fresh flowers on every table to the colorful wallpaper. It had a true homey feel.

"I've never been here," Abby said, opening her menu. "What would you suggest?"

"They do everything well. You can't go wrong."

Abby heard a squeal, and then a sturdy woman with silver-black hair and a wide smile came over. "I can't believe it." She bent down and kissed and hugged Jason. "It's been too long." She turned to Abby. "I'm Rosemary."

"Hello, I'm Abby."

She bent down and hugged her. "Any friend of Jason's is a friend of mine. Do you mind if I borrow him for one moment?"

"No. You have a wonderful place here."

"Thank you," she said, her smile widening. "Jason, come."

Jason followed Rosemary over to a corner. "Don't embarrass me," he told her in a hushed voice. She was one of his mother's best friends, and he'd bought the small Baltimore restaurant for her.

"I won't, but please let me enjoy this moment," she said, fanning herself as if she expected to faint. "I never thought you'd do this. Is she the one?"

He nodded. He'd never brought another woman to this place.

"She's a little on the skinny side. How long have you known her?"

"Not long."

"What does she do?"

"She's a consultant."

"She looks like she makes good money."

Jason shook his head with a smile. "You don't need to ask me all the questions."

"I'm only asking the questions your mother would if she were here. I promised I'd look after you when she's not around."

"She's in another county, not on another planet. Besides, you've done fine so far." His mother lived in Fredrick County, several miles away from Montgomery County, where he lived.

"But you had me worried."

"There's nothing to worry about now."

"Let me go find—"

"Not yet. I don't want to overwhelm her. I haven't made anything official yet."

Rosemary paused, cautious. "You mean she doesn't know about us?"

"No."

"How much does she know about you?"

"As much as I want to share." He lightly kissed her on the cheek. "Please, I have to go, but I wanted to see you."

"Come over later. And don't you groan at me. I want to know what you've been up to."

Jason walked back to his table, wondering if he'd made the right choice. But it felt right. He liked Abby the more he got to know her. She hadn't flinched. She hadn't grinned. She'd shown no reaction to the revelation about his background and how others saw him, and he was glad. It had been awkward telling her how he felt, but she didn't seem to judge him. Just like Gwen hadn't judged him.

He liked her. He didn't want to, but he did. She annoyed him, but she didn't make him angry. He liked to see her cool facade shaken. He didn't want to be treated like some kind of clinical trial, which she seemed determined to do with her attempt at distancing. He didn't want to be put into the same category as all the other clients she worked with. With her, he wanted to be different. He wanted her to see him. It had been a long time since he'd been attracted to any woman—since he'd made work his life. For the first time, she'd made him interested in something else.

"Sorry about that," Jason said, taking a seat at the table.

"Don't be. But this doesn't fit."

"What do you mean?"

"How can I help you if you take me to a place where people love you?"

"I just thought you should know that I'm not all bad."

"I didn't think you were. But so far, I'm still not sure you need my services. I did at first, but now…"

"Now I've changed your mind?"

She narrowed her eyes. "I think that's what you want. I think you like being a—"

His gaze darkened. "No, I don't," he said before she could finish her statement.

"You still haven't told me what someone said to make you seek me out."

"You know enough."

"Your table manners are fine. I know about your temper but have yet to see it." She paused. "Wait, yes, I have."

"You have? When?"

"I was at—" She stopped when she saw an older man enter with an attractive woman on his arm. A younger, prettier woman.

Abby immediately thought of her ex and how, after he had admitted to her that he'd fallen in love with another woman, initially she had felt a little sorry for him. She could understand his feelings changing and fell for his tears—that was, until the divorce. All that she'd helped him build belonged to him. He'd followed the prenuptial agreement to the letter and offered her nothing. She'd hated him for a while until she developed an ulcer and decided to forget him and get her life back. The life she had before she'd become a successful CEO's wife.

But as she looked across the room, for a moment, she felt wounded and lost. She'd been willing to give Charles a second chance. She'd known that a man as powerful as Charles would have many women interested in him; and there had been cracks in their marriage, so she could understand his wandering eye. She'd wanted to be understanding. But that hadn't been enough. That was what had hurt the most. She'd been willing to work on the marriage, but he'd said it was over. That he didn't love her anymore. It was at that moment she'd wondered if he'd ever loved her.

Why couldn't he at least have been grateful? Why had he treated their marriage like a business transaction that had gone sour? Why had he used her, and why had she let herself be used? Had he ever loved her as much as she'd loved him?

"Abby?"

She turned to Jason. "I'm sorry, I lost my train of thought."

"Do you know the woman or man?" he asked, noticing her looking at the couple.

Abby sighed. "No. They just remind me of my ex and his new fiancée. But that's not your problem."

"Let's switch seats."

"Why?"

"Just move."

She did. Then she saw Jason look past her, and a predatory expression crossed his face. "What?"

"Give me your hand," he said without looking at her.

She did, and he took it, drew it to his mouth and kissed it. "How long have you been divorced?"

"Five years."

He looked at her, surprised. "Really? I would think you would be over him by now."

"Me, too."

"Why did you leave him?"

"I didn't leave him, he left me."

The look of fun left Jason's face. "He left you?"

"Yes."

"For some young wind-up toy?"

"Jason, that's not a nice thing to say."

"I'm not trying to be nice. I'm trying to make you feel better. Tell me. Were you married at the time?"

"Yes."

"Were you separated then?"

"No."

"As I said, he left you for some new wind-up toy." Jason stood, leaned over, then kissed her on the mouth and whispered in her ear, "I want you to close your eyes for a moment."

Abby wasn't sure what he was up to, but she was game. She closed her eyes and sat there feeling very vulnerable and a little nervous. "Now, open your eyes." When she did, she was delighted to see a large bowl of delicious fruit in front of her.

"I asked Rosa to prepare a special dish just for you."

After finishing the bowl of fruit, followed by a delicious meal of Southern deep-fried chicken, buttered collard greens, homemade spicy corn bread and fresh peach pie, Abby folded her napkin on the table. "Jason, I recently heard something about someone accusing you of accosting them. What did you do?" she asked. Judith had conveniently shared this bit of information with Abby, although she didn't know why.

Jason gritted his teeth. "I didn't do anything."

"I know. I believe you."

He blinked. "You believe me?"

"Yes. Not everyone falls prey to the machinations of the business class. I don't believe every story I hear, especially about certain people."

"Since you seem to know so much about me, and I'm sure you've done your homework, why haven't you brought up the fact that I was in prison yet?"

"Because it was overturned, and it doesn't matter. You were innocent."

Jason was quiet for a long time.

"I have to come back here again. The food is wonderful."

"Rosa would love to hear that."

"I'd love to tell her," Abby said, then she saw Rosemary and waved, but Rosemary looked preoccupied and didn't see her. "I guess she's busy."

"You'll tell her when we come back," Jason said, then took the bill and walked over to the cashier before she could reply.

Abby knew it was presumptuous of him to think they'd come here again, but she had a feeling they would, and she looked forward to it. She saw Jason disappear to the back of the restaurant, then reappear looking solemn.

"Is everything okay?"

"Hmm," Jason said, helping her with her jacket.

Abby knew he wouldn't reveal much else, so she let the topic drop.

"You really believe me?" Jason asked as they left the restaurant and walked to their cars.

"Yes," Abby said, taking out her keys. Although the calendar said November, it didn't feel like it yet. A mild wind toyed with the hem of her skirt, and she pulled her coat tighter. "Why are you so amazed?"

"Because few people do."

"People are too afraid to, that's all. Everyone knows that if something had really happened, you'd still be in prison. Her smearing your reputation was just payback for something. No one has the courage to call her a liar, and like I said before, you're easy prey."

He stopped walking. "Prey?" he said in an absent tone.

Abby halted, then turned and looked at him. She saw him glance away, then look at her. She wondered if he was practicing not looking straight at her. "A scapegoat. You intimidate people. You do your own thing. That's what I don't understand. What didn't you do? If she's the woman Judith told me about, I've met her. She doesn't like hearing the word no."

Jason lifted a brow, then looked away and shoved his hands in his pockets.

Abby nodded as she put the pieces together. He'd made an enemy of a powerful woman. "I also haven't seen your famous temper yet." At least, not up close and personal.

He sent her a glance, then looked away again and frowned. "Don't worry," he said in a low voice. "You're about to."

Chapter 6

Jason had sensed something was wrong when he'd seen Rosemary's face, and then she'd spoken to him and lied that things were okay. But the happy woman he was used to had appeared tense. It had been luck that forced him to park his car near the alley where they kept the trash bins. He was looking in that direction when he caught a glimpse of two men holding her husband, Henry, against the wall.

"So, where is it?" one of the men asked.

Henry held his hands up. "I don't know."

"Where's—?"

"He hasn't been back in days," Henry cut in.

"You better not be lying to us." He lifted his fist, ready to strike him.

Jason didn't allow him to finish. Within minutes, the two thugs were running down the alley as if escaping a pack of dogs. "Why didn't you tell me you needed to take out trash?" Jason said, brushing some dirt off his shoes. He helped Henry get up off the ground and then leaned against the wall. "I thought things were going well, and then I find you going through a shakedown."

"I don't know what's going on. I just needed a little extra cash. Business was getting into some trouble, so I signed with a new partner, some guy by the name of Old Man Taylor, then I have those two guys asking about wanting their money."

Jason sighed. "Why didn't you tell me you needed money?"

"Everybody comes to you for money. Besides, it didn't seem like a big deal."

"You know who those two guys work for, right?"

"I didn't at first. Then Old Man Taylor told me he was in deep with Blues Man. I'm scared. I haven't told Rosemary yet."

"Let me see the contract you have with him. We'll get you out of it, and I'll find a way to settle your account."

"It's dangerous."

"You're family," he said, resting his hand on the older man's shoulder.

"I feel like such a fool." Henry looked down and saw blood dripping on to Jason's shoes. "You got cut."

"I got clumsy," Jason said, dismissing his concern. "Don't worry about it. Just get me what I asked. Only deal with me from now on."

"Let Rosemary clean you up."

"You want her asking questions?" Jason asked, already knowing the answer. "I just need you to do something for me."

"Tell the lady you had to go?"

"Yes."

"At least let your lady look after you."

Jason shook his head. "It's not like that."

"She's not going to be happy."

"I'll make it up to her."

Henry sighed. "Too late, she's coming over here."

"You should have stayed back," Jason said, annoyed that Abby was there.

"I did, but now the threat's gone. I got their license plate."

"Thanks." He took the piece of paper from her and put it in his jacket pocket. He didn't need to look at the number or give it to the police; he knew who the men were.

Abby reached for him. "You're bleeding."

He took a step back. "I'm fine. We'll finish this meeting later."

"You should see a doctor."

"I'll call you."

"Will you just listen?"

He continued to walk away. She turned to Henry. "Is he always this stubborn?"

"Yes. Make sure to check on him after a day or two. I don't mean to burden you, but I can't tell my wife about this."

"Why not? He just helped save your life."

"I know, but if she finds out what this fight was about, then she'll tell his mom and he'll give me hell for that."

Abby sighed. "He won't be happy to see me."

"I'll give you three free meals."

The thought of another meal of Southern fried chicken with buttered collard greens and homemade corn bread changed her mind. "You're on."

A half hour later, Jason walked into an old building. In an exquisitely furnished room on the first floor was a large ornate desk. He sat down. The man on the other side of the desk smiled at him. Blues Man was a few years older than Jason and a little heavier, his brown eyes always shielded by dark sunglasses.

"Hello, cousin," he said in a friendly tone.

Jason didn't match the tone or the smile. His jaw twitched. "Southern Taste is off-limits."

"It was until they went into business with Old Man Taylor."

"They didn't know he was connected to you."

"They do now."

"How much does he owe?"

Blues Man shook his head. "You were always so serious. Aren't you going to ask me how I am?"

"I'll ask when I start to care. How much?"

Blues Man adjusted his dark sunglasses and gave him a figure.

Jason nodded. "I'll cover it."

"The usual way?"

"How else?"

"You know, there's no point in trying to protect your image. From what I hear, people wash their hands after they touch your money."

Jason stood. "We're done here."

"I could do much more for you. At least I get respect. You're smart, and look at how you're treated. I'm feared and revered. You could be the same. You'll never fit in with them. They'll smile to your face and stab you in the back. Haven't the last few years taught you that?"

"I'm not you."

"Pity. You'd be a lot more powerful if you were."

Jason headed for the door.

"Who was that lady you were with?"

He spun around, his voice hard. "You leave her out of this."

Blues Man held his hands up in surrender. "I'm just asking a friendly question."

"She's none of your business."

"I can't help being curious. You haven't had a companion in a long time. Shame what happened to the last one."

"You stay away from her."

"It's a dangerous world out there. I could keep her safe."

"You know I don't make threats."

"You're out of your league again. Be careful, cuz."

Henry sat in his office and wiped his forehead. It had been a close call. He hadn't expected to have things fall apart. The business had fallen on hard times, and Rosemary trusted him with the books. She didn't know anything. He didn't want her to worry, so he had taken a loan from the one man he shouldn't have. Jason had warned him, but Old Man Taylor had made the prospect sound solid. He'd gotten in deep, and before he knew it, it was too late. He'd expected to get his kneecaps broken today and then beg Rosemary for forgiveness. Jason had been a godsend, but he knew the trouble wasn't over. Jason had gotten hurt because of him, and if anything happened to him, he knew Rosemary wouldn't forgive him. And she was one of the best things to happen in his life.

He'd been lucky that the woman with Jason had agreed not to tell Rosemary, and he hoped she'd keep her promise and look in on him to make sure he was all right. While he didn't see him as a son, Jason was a young man he admired who had also taken his son, Benjamin—Benny, for short—under his wing and mentored him. Henry had finally improved his life and that of his son, and he didn't want anything to ruin it.

Although he appeared brash at times, Jason had been exceptionally patient with his son and had been like a big brother to him. He'd been there for him while he finished middle school and high school, and when he went off to college in Florida, all thanks to Jason's help and effort. He only needed a couple more weeks, then he could pay back his debt. Henry jumped when the phone rang. He wiped his forehead once more, then answered with trembling hands.

"You're a lucky man," a voice said in an amused tone.

Henry swallowed. The man he had to deal with was rarely amused. He didn't know how to act. Was he going to mention the loan? He decided to play dumb. "I am?"

"Jason was just here. I thought you told me he was out of this." Blues Man wasn't pleased.

Jason wasn't supposed to know of their dealings. That had been one of the stipulations, which was why he had used Old Man Taylor's name, instead of telling Jason he had been dealing directly with Blues Man. "I didn't expect him to be here."

"Are you sure? We both know that Old Man Taylor was just a cover for your wife, in case she overheard anything. I did that as a courtesy because I like her. But we both know you were the one with the debt."

"I'll get you the money."

"Like I said, you're a lucky man. Jason took care of it."

"All of it?"

"Every. Last. Cent."

"Damn."

"I was caught off guard. I don't usually have family drop in and take care of my clients' debts. You know I don't mix family with business. It makes things messy, and I don't like things being messy."

"I didn't mean to. I swear. Rosemary and I were shocked to see him. He hadn't come by in a while, and then he brought a date."

"Sure. I believe you. But only this once. However, you mess with me next time, and my cousin won't be able to help you. I don't like anyone who uses my family ties against me. I respect my cousin and he respects me. He and Aunt Beatrice are all I've got. I won't let anyone ruin that. Is that clear?"

"Yes."

Then silence fell. Henry wiped his brow again. He could feel his palms go sweaty. Blues Man was a cold character. Unlike Jason, there was no soft core. Blues Man felt for no one but his family.

"Is there something else?" Henry asked when the silence deepened.

"I'm waiting for you to expand on my cousin's visit."

"Expand?"

Blues Man sighed, as if he thought Henry were dense. "What was he doing there?"

"Eating."

"Are you trying to get on my nerves?"

"No, no," Henry said, stumbling over his words. "Never. I wouldn't—"

"You mentioned a woman."

"Yeah, right..." Henry said, relieved that he was no longer of interest.

"On a date?"

"It looked that way. I mean, he's never brought anyone here before. And he talked to Rosemary about her. I didn't hear much, but she told me he looked happy.

Blues Man swore. "Jason looked happy? Stop messing with me."

"I'm serious."

"What's her name?"

"I don't know."

"Your wife will. Keep me informed."

She didn't want to go, but she'd made a promise. And she felt guilty. Instead of one day, it had been two, and it was only after Jason had an associate call and cancel his appointment that Abby decided to check in on him.

She was afraid to. Seeing him fight hadn't frightened her. Even his curt tone when she'd asked about what had happened hadn't scared her. But when he moved away from her attempt to touch him, that had hurt. It had unnerved her. She knew he wouldn't like her showing up on his doorstep, concerned. He was the type that didn't like to be fussed over. She'd take his rudeness and leave and never make a promise like that again. She still thought of the brief touch of his lips on hers in the restaurant.

Abby knocked, and a large wooden door opened. A young man in his early twenties answered. "Dad said you would come," he greeted her, opening the door wide, relief clear on his face. "My name's Benny." Abby saw little similarity between the young man and Henry, except for the fear in his eyes. "He won't eat. He won't drink. It's bad this time."

This time? How many fights had he gotten into? "Okay," Abby said, keeping her voice calm. "Is he asleep?"

"He goes in and out."

That didn't sound good, but she wasn't really alarmed. Although Henry had sounded worried, she didn't think he had been seriously wounded. But the moment she walked into the bedroom, she knew she was wrong. Abby rushed over to Jason. He was as hot as a sauna, and he lay on the bed covered in sweat, his breathing labored. She stared down at him in shock and concern. "When was the last time you checked on him?"

"This morning."

She turned to Benny. "He's been like this since morning, and you haven't called an ambulance?"

"He wouldn't let me."

She looked down at Jason and said in a grim tone, "Call an ambulance. He can't fight you now."

Jason grabbed her arm and said in a low voice, "Yes, I can."

Chapter 7

"You're going to the hospital," Abby said, quickly recovering from her shock.

Jason released his hold on her arm and said in a tired but firm tone, "No, I'm not."

She leaned over him and reached for his arm. "Let me see your wound."

"No." He shoved her away.

Abby stumbled back, surprised by his casual strength, then steeled herself and went over to the other side of the bed. "Let me see it."

"I said no. Go away." He shoved her away, harder this time.

She looked up at Benny. "Call the ambulance."

"No."

She grabbed Jason's pinkie. "Don't make me do this."

His lip curled. "You wouldn't. I'm a sick man, remember?"

"Exactly. That's why you're going to the hospital."

"No, I'm not."

"I don't want to have to change your mind."

"You won't."

She shoved his pinkie back. Hard.

He swore.

"You'll pay me a hundred later. Now I'll break your pinkie if you don't start listening to me. Lie still so that I can see your wound." She pushed the pinkie back a little in warning. "Agreed?"

He swore again.

"Two hundred. Is that a yes?"

Jason bit his lip and nodded.

Abby released his finger and unwound the bandage that was wrapped around his arm. The wound was swollen and discolored. Her stomach turned, and she softly swore.

Jason looked at her, stunned. "You can swear, and I can't?"

"Yes," she said, in no mood to argue. She pointed to his injury. "This is why men die early—because they're stupid. It's infected. Why didn't you have someone look at it?"

"I thought it was fine."

"Liar. It's not like you can't afford health care. Is it pride? God, this is disgusting. It looks like it's eating your flesh, too. You must be in a lot of pain."

He shot her a glance. "Right now, you're the biggest pain."

"I'm surprised you can still joke about this." She knew he had to be hurting bad.

He shook his head. "I'm not joking. Go away."

"Who can I call for you?"

He grabbed her arm again and pulled her down close to him. "I said get out."

She boldly stared back at him. "You must be sick, because you're not thinking straight right now. You're a bastard, and you can't fight me even though you think you can. Because right now, you don't have the strength. You're not in the position to tell me what to do."

"Do you think I'll let you grab my pinkie again?"

She let her gaze travel to his boxer shorts, then returned it to his face. "No, I won't grab your pinkie. This time I'll grab something else that I know is a lot bigger than your pinkie, so that you'll get the message."

Jason flashed a seductive grin. "Are you trying to turn me on?"

Abby blinked, her tone flat. "If I grab you, you won't be smiling."

Jason rolled away from her and pulled himself up off the bed, cradling his arm and swearing fiercely.

Abby grinned from the other side of the bed. "Oh, I'm going to make a lot of money today."

He shot her a glance. "Are you out of your mind?"

"Maybe." She stood, not liking how pale he looked. "Lie down or you'll faint."

"Men don't faint," Jason said, swaying a little.

"Pass out, then. I don't care. I just know that you're too big for me to catch you."

He sat back down on the bed and rested against the headboard. She knew he was holding himself up by sheer will. Beads of sweat pooled on his forehead, and his lips had lost their color. "You're so stubborn." She rested her hands on her hips. "I don't like you right now, and maybe it's your time to go. You could already have sepsis or gangrene, I don't know, but you're still a client and I want to give you a chance. You don't trust me, but I'll tell you this—I don't want anything from you. I won't use this to my advantage. I won't let anyone know if you don't want me to. But I will help you. And you will accept my help. You're not okay. If you were, you would have thrown me out by now, but you can hardly lift your head. You can get mad at me later. I'm not going to let you die when I've just started to like you."

Abby could tell Jason had heard her because he'd opened his mouth to respond, but at that moment, she heard the ambulance drive up; then the EMTs rushed into the bedroom.

Beatrice cleaned up her dinner dishes, still unable to believe her conversation with Rosemary.

"Guess who came into the restaurant?" she had said with an enthusiasm Beatrice hadn't heard in a long time.

"You know I hate guessing."

"Guess anyway."

"The president?"

"Your son."

Beatrice shook her head, annoyed. "So? He's come there before."

"But never with a woman."

Beatrice sat up with interest. "Are you sure?"

"Yes, I saw them, and he told me that she's the one."

"Who is she? What is she like?"

"She's pretty, a little too skinny and uptight, but I'll take care of that. He says she's a consultant. Don't know what kind yet, but I'll get to the bottom of things."

"I don't believe this."

"If I hadn't seen it for myself, I wouldn't either. But the best thing was—he looked happy."

Beatrice couldn't breathe. She didn't remember the last time Jason was happy. She felt tears sting her eyes, but she was also cautious. She didn't want to get her hopes up too high. "How long has he been seeing her? Why would he keep her a secret?"

"You know him. He's cagey, but I'm sure you'll meet

her soon. From what I can guess, they haven't known each other for very long."

"Why do you say that?"

"Because he said she's not aware of how he feels about her. She's clueless about his intentions, like a two-year-old with a hundred dollar bill."

"I don't know if I should be glad or worried."

"Be glad for now. We can always worry later. I just thought you should know."

"Thanks." She was in a fog the rest of the day. Who was this woman who'd made her son happy? Who had been able to convince him to take her to Rosemary's restaurant? Things must be serious. She knew that getting Jason to re-create his image was a good idea, but she'd never expected this. And so soon. Maybe good things would finally begin to happen in his life. She still hated how he'd never let her see him when he had been in prison, and he still wouldn't talk about it. After Gwen's death, he rarely talked about much. She hated how he hurt in silence, but he'd done that since he was a young man. She wanted to meet this woman and thank her, but she knew she needed to give them space. Give him time. She hoped this woman was the right one. But at least he was giving relationships a second chance. She'd been certain he'd made his work his only mistress.

Then the phone rang, and just like she feared, Beatrice had her hopes crushed.

She had actually hurt him. Jason lay in the hospital bed, still in shock. She'd used force—violence. On *him.* He couldn't wait to see her again and give her a piece of his mind. He had a long list of things to tell her. He'd practiced in his mind what he was going to say and how he was going to say it. Unfortunately, he never had a chance to. It had been two days, and she hadn't come to visit him yet. She'd been so adamant that he had to go to the hospital. Why hadn't she come to see how he was doing? It had been a close call, and he owed her his life. He hated owing anyone. It had been bad enough that he'd gone to her for help in the first place, and now he was indebted to her. And he still liked her. A lot. That annoyed him the most. It annoyed him that he'd listened for her footsteps every second of the day. That he wanted to hear her voice. That he liked that she wasn't afraid of him and didn't want anything from him.

At that moment, the door opened, and one of the nurses entered. "Oh, you're awake. Did you see her?"

"Her?"

"Oh, I'm sorry. I forgot. She only likes to come and visit you when you're asleep. She told the staff that she didn't want to bother you."

Jason smiled. She had come. She was hiding from him. Two could play this game.

Chapter 8

He even looked fierce sleeping, Abby thought as she stood by Jason's hospital bedside. She glanced at the collection of colorful flowers on the windowsill from Henry and Rosemary, and his mother. As she continued looking at him, she saw no gentleness, just a hard presence. She felt as if she had come upon a sleeping bear one approached with caution. She was glad that he would be okay and wondered if he'd thank her or stop seeing her.

She really didn't want to lose him as a client. Not just for the loss of revenue, but for the challenge. She liked him, although she wasn't sure why. She could do so much to help him, and he wasn't too bad to look at. She sized up the entire length of him. He was beautifully made. She lifted her gaze, looked at his face and saw two brown eyes looking back at her. She gasped and jumped back. "You're awake."

He sat up and grinned. "It would seem so."

She swallowed. "How do you feel?"

He motioned her closer. She shook her head.

"Why are you so far away?" he teased. "You think I'll bite you?"

"Are you still angry?"

He turned and stared up at the ceiling.

"You were really sick."

She saw his eyes drift close. She moved in closer.

"Is the medicine taking effect?"

When he didn't respond, Abby waited a full minute, then breathed a sigh of relief. "At least you'll rest." She pulled up the sheet that had fallen away. He seized her hand.

Abby let out a squeal and tried to yank herself free. "Stop that."

Jason tightened his hold. "You'll pay for putting me in here."

"I saved your life."

"I know." He pulled her down and kissed her—quick, hard…amazing. When he drew away, it was with such speed Abby wasn't sure she could believe her senses. Her mind spun, her breath quickened, her heart raced. Had he really kissed her, or had it been her imagination? Her lips continued to burn. But it had been too fast; she found herself staring at his lips, wanting more. Wanting to make sure it was real. That he felt this fierce attraction as much as she did. Or was he just toying with her? She hadn't been able to read him yet. She couldn't trust his motives. She looked at him. He'd turned his face from her. She found herself wanting to touch his hair, to stroke his face, to soothe him. But she couldn't.

"What?" she asked when she heard him mumble something.

He turned to her. "I really hate being in your debt."

"You're not."

"Of course I am. If you ever need anything, just let me know."

He said the words with such intensity, she felt heat steel into her cheeks. "First, you'll have to stop fighting."

"What?"

"You'll have to find another way to do business without fighting. From what I learned about you from Henry, you've gotten into fights before."

He rubbed his chin. "It's been a while."

"Well, it has to stop."

His brow rose up a fraction. "It wasn't on my to-do list."

"Who were those men?"

"The matter is settled. Forget it."

"But—"

He pressed a finger against her lips. "I'll indulge you when it comes to other things, but not this. You'll never mention this again. You'll never speak of those men again. You'll forget the make of their car and the number of their license plate. Do you understand me? Don't speak, just nod your head." His eyes pierced into hers.

She did. He removed his hand. "Good. Now, I really am tired. Don't come back here."

"What?"

"I'm fine. You don't need to worry about me. I'll see you in your office."

"But—"

He held up his hand before she could speak. "I mean it. Don't come back here." He lowered his gaze and softened his tone. "I don't like you seeing me like this." His gaze met hers, pleading. "Okay?"

"All right." She handed him a slip.

"What's this?"

"How much you owe me for swearing."

He looked at the amount written down on the paper, then swore.

Abby took out a pen from her handbag. "Let me add to that," she said with a little grin.

Jason crumbled up the paper and threw it across the room. "I was sick. They shouldn't count."

"All right. I'll let you get away with it this time." Abby picked up the paper, tore it up and put it in the wastebasket. "See you at the office."

At least he hadn't fired her. But she had to figure out what those two men were about. She couldn't have Jason getting in trouble again if she was to clean up his image. Thankfully nothing had been written up in the paper or mentioned on the local news about an assault at Southern Taste. She called Henry.

"I just spoke to Jason, and he won't tell me what those men wanted. He wants me to forget what I saw."

"That's a good idea."

"Unfortunately, I can't. Especially when what happens to him affects my business."

"Your business?"

"Yes, every aspect of Jason's life is my concern, especially if he may have to meet up with men like that in the future. What's going on?"

"You should listen to Jason and leave it alone. It won't happen again."

"Does Rosemary know?"

"No."

"Well, she will if you don't start talking."

Henry sighed.

"Let me guess. The restaurant's in trouble, and you wanted to find a way to get money fast."

"Yes."

"How bad were things?"

"Pretty bad. I didn't know how much longer we could

last. My son had even been giving me some of the money he made working for Jason as an assistant, but it wasn't enough."

"That certainly isn't sustainable. He shouldn't have to. Okay, let me help you."

"No, you don't need to worry, everything's been taken care of."

"How? By who?" Abby was curious and had a sinking feeling she knew who had probably stepped in to help, but she didn't want to make any assumptions. She decided to make Henry sweat a little more.

"You need to let Rosemary know what you've been up to, and right now."

"Why so soon?"

"Because I'll be coming by in one hour to get my free meal. Be ready."

Abby was there in forty-five minutes, and placed an order for their signature jambalaya.

"How are you doing?" Rosemary said, coming out to greet her.

Abby resisted the urge to lick her fingers. "I just came from seeing Jason. Eating this meal is lifting my spirits."

"Yes." Rosemary laughed. "That one could put any woman in a bad mood."

"He doesn't want to see me, or rather, not while he's in the hospital."

"He's a proud man with a lot of bad memories."

"He's giving me a few of my own."

Rosemary smiled. "But you like him."

"He's a client," Abby said, not wanting Rosemary to get the wrong impression. She changed the subject. "This jambalaya is delicious."

"Thank you."

Abby pretended to look around the place with interest. She'd chosen a booth away from the other guests so that she'd be able to talk to Rosemary without being overheard. "How come the place isn't more crowded?"

Rosemary's expression fell, and she took a seat. "You must be psychic or something because Henry just told me some bad news."

"What?"

"I don't know if I should—"

"Jason may not be able to help you right now, but I can. Please, tell me."

"Business has been slow the past few years."

"Years?"

Rosemary looked around and lowered her voice. "Yes, although my husband didn't want to face it until it's too late."

"It's not too late. And there's no reason your business shouldn't be doing better."

"People had warned me that having a restaurant was a cutthroat business. Maybe I dreamed too much."

"The location, the decor and the food are stellar. However…" Abby looked around with a critical eye. "It's none of my business," she said with false modesty.

"Please, I want to hear what you have to say."

"The wait staff needs new uniforms. They approach the table in a lackluster style that can ruin one's appetite. You need some color and liveliness and a hint of the South, without it being caricature. Also, twice I heard someone ask to speak with the chef, to compliment him, and the offer was refused."

"He's a busy man."

"I don't care. Tell him to make the time. Also, some of the items on the menu need to be changed."

"What do you mean?"

"Updated. You know. Like, the pulled pork dish could be fancied up by adding some more spice and color. I believe a few key adjustments will make a big difference."

"I would love to see things turn around."

"And I'd like to help," Abby said, surprised by her own eagerness. Jason was a hard case, but helping Rosemary and Henry turn their business around would be easier. She thought for a moment. And helping a business, not just a person, successfully change its image would help expand her portfolio. It would be a skill that Judith couldn't follow—at least, not for now. "I know of a woman who is excellent at making customized uniforms. I'll talk to her and send you some ideas. Okay?"

"How much—"

Abby waved the thought away. "Just give me another order of this, and I'm fine." She pointed to her empty plate.

"I'm so glad Jason brought you here. You're good for him."

"I'm not sure he believes that, at least not yet."

Rosemary winked. "He'll find out soon enough."

"You do this just to annoy me," Beatrice said, arranging the flowers on the windowsill in Jason's hospital room. "You want to make me upset. You know I hate these places."

"It's been a long time."

"Not long enough. I'll never forget the last time you were in here. I thought you'd never come out."

Jason smiled. "You can't keep a good man down."

"What was it about?"

His smile fell. "Nothing."

"You're not doing anything—"

"I was helping a friend, that's all."

"Your cousin called me."

Jason stiffened. He didn't take his cousin for a snitch. He swore. "What did he want?"

"He wanted to know more about this lady you're seeing."

Jason pulled at his sheets, annoyed. "He'll find out when I tell him."

"You haven't even told me yet."

"It happened faster than I thought."

"How's the consultation going?"

Jason laughed, then grimaced. "She wants me to stop fighting."

"Glad to hear she has some sense."

"You haven't met her yet?" he asked, surprised that they'd missed each other.

"No. But she's right. If you want to change, you have to change everything."

"Sure."

Her voice grew more intense. She lightly touched the side of his face. "When are you going to stop fighting against the world? Fighting against something makes you weak. When will you start fighting *for* something? All your life you're fighting against your background, poverty, disrespect. You can relax now and just stand for something. That's what Gwen would have wanted."

"If I were as good as her, I wouldn't still be alive."

"That night wasn't your fault." Beatrice suddenly looked tired and sat down in the chair beside his bed.

He straightened. "Are you okay?"

"Sugar level is a little low."

"Let me call the nurse to get you some orange juice."

"You know what I would love? To take Bill on a vacation."

William "Big Bill" Wallace was one of his mother's

oldest friends, who had a major kidney disease and had to get dialysis several times a week, making travel difficult.

"You know I can pay for the top care if you wanted."

"I know." She sighed. "But it would be nice to have a place where Big Bill could go and not have to worry about his health."

He knew his mother worried about a lot of things, but he didn't want her worrying about him anymore. "I won't let you down this time."

"You've never let me down. I just want more for you." She left.

Jason thought about what his mother had said the next morning, eager to be discharged from the hospital. Today was his final day.

"Sorry to see you go," a nurse said, coming into the room. "I'm glad I got a chance to see you. I had to see what Abby's man was like."

He looked up at her, surprised and pleased. "Abby's man?"

"Yes, you're a celebrity here because of her. Everyone made sure you got the best care."

"I thought it was because of my money."

"That doesn't matter around here. We can still make your life miserable. But we looked after you because of her. We all adore her. She's the sweetest, kindest, most caring person I've ever met."

Were they talking about the same woman? "Abby Baylor?"

"Yes."

The nurse was called away before he could ask any more questions. Jason changed into his street clothes, and then walked out to the main hospital area. Over on one side of the wall, he saw a series of awards, and her name was on top. "It's nice to see you up and about," a nurse said. She was the one who'd helped him before. "Are you looking for Abby?"

"She's here?"

"Yes, every Wednesday. Come on."

She took Jason up to the neonatal ward, where he saw Abby cradling a tiny little baby. "She holds the preemies. Many of the parents aren't able to come in as often as they like or need to. The babies really blossom under her attention. She also holds clothing drives so that we can get caps and clothes for them. Because they are so small, we can't buy the right items. Most of their clothes need to be made." The nurse went on to explain that Abby had started volunteering at the hospital during high school and continued all through college, and even after she got married. She was there every week, unless she was traveling out of town. They could always rely on her dependability and tireless efforts.

Jason stared in awe. So this was who she really was. Here she was, giving without needing anything in return. It was a selfless act to help babies who would never remember her. Families who may never know her name, or the number of hours she'd spent holding their little ones. But she was helping, and it was beautiful.

At that moment Jason wasn't sure about himself. His mother's words in the hospital had shown him another side of himself. He was like some hungry, grasping animal. He'd become a creature who gave to no one, who only thought of himself and gaining more power, respect. He'd been angry for so long, he didn't know what peace felt like. That's when he realized he didn't want to be that man anymore. He wanted to be the possibility Abby saw. He wanted to do more. Be more. He could really help others. False hollow victories—he didn't need them anymore. He wanted to give like Abby. He wanted his life to matter and make a difference. To feel that serene peace that she had on her face. He'd never felt that. He'd always felt empty. He was ashamed of his life. All the wealth meant nothing.

He passed by one of the hospital rooms and heard a couple crying. Maybe they had no baby to take home with them, and the possibility of their pain washed over him like a wave. He had isolated himself from these realities. He knew how it felt to leave a hospital without the one you loved. He'd had to leave without Gwen. He still remembered waking up, staring at his mother and Blues Man and asking about Gwen, and them avoiding his eyes and he knew. Before they'd even told him, he knew. She was gone. The woman he'd planned to spend the rest of his life with was gone. Taken away in a blaze of bullets.

Afterward, work and money had been his addiction. Others turned to women and wine, but, no, he'd wanted a high that others could see. That others would revere. That others would respect. That's all he'd wanted, and he had achieved that.

But it didn't matter anymore. He suddenly realized that the world was so much bigger than his pain had been, and there were those who were helpless and needed others to look after them. Like Big Bill, who couldn't travel because he needed his dialysis in order to live, and the babies, who were too weak to survive on their own and needed to be held by people like Abby, and the couple who needed the strength to move forward.

That's when he decided he wanted to do something more with the business he now owned. What if his resorts provided the kind of service that would allow people like his mother's friend to go on vacation, and for a time, forget about their illnesses and limitations, to live without feeling as if they were sick or invalids? Yes, kids with major catastrophic illnesses could go on vacation made possible by programs such as the Make-A-Wish Foundation, but what about adults? What about those living with lifelong illnesses, who were not facing imminent death, but had dreams of traveling and having fun, just like anyone else. He'd have to get the right partners, but he was determined to make a real difference. Be a new man. At that moment, he felt as if he could really dream again. Something he'd been afraid to do for too long.

Dare he hope once more to have a family of his own? To have a woman who would stand by his side and give her heart to him? A woman who trusted him? A woman he could trust in return?

He knew the first moment he'd seen her that he'd wanted Abby, but it had been in a greedy way. He had wanted to possess her. Now he knew his feelings were much more. As he watched her, he knew she was the safety and beauty he'd sought after losing Gwen. What she had was intangible. Her outer beauty was evident, but in the quiet of the hospital room, dressed in the bland gown, with a small, ill baby in her arms, she looked magnificent, like shimmering gold, her heart revealed with every gentle touch. Could he persuade a woman like her to be with him? He knew his money wouldn't be enough, and that prospect scared him. It had been his armor and shield. Most of the women hadn't seen past his wealth, and those who did only wanted to remind him that he should be grateful. He would have to be strategic. He would let her help him change and learn how to steal her heart.

Chapter 9

Abby looked out the car window up at the white early December sky and felt a faint glimmer of hope. Jason had fully recovered from his injury, but their session today hadn't gone well. She had taken him to volunteer at a community event, where a man had been so disruptive that Jason had lost his temper and shouted at him, which had then led to a rather unpleasant scene with Jason using a few choice words and owing her a total of five hundred dollars. Now they sat in his car as he drove them back to her office.

"Pull over," Abby said.

"Why?"

"Just do it."

He did.

Abby jumped out of the car. "Look, it's snowing." The snowflakes fell like white petals all around them.

"So?"

"It's the first snow of the year. You should enjoy it. Go on. Catch one on your tongue."

"Do I look five years old to you?"

"Come on, it's fun."

Jason got out, leaned against the car and shook his head. "No."

Abby shrugged, stuck out her tongue and caught a snowflake.

He folded his arms and sent her an odd look.

"Don't you love when it snows?" she asked him, hoping to remove the dark look on his face.

"I rarely pay attention."

"How about as a kid? Did you love it then?"

"Snow just meant we were going to be cold," he said softly. He glanced away and stared up at the sky, a look of pain crossing his face.

Abby regretted her question. She'd forgotten about his childhood. His bio had mentioned a rags-to-riches existence, but she'd been so in awe of the riches he now had that she'd never asked him about his past. What it might have been like. She'd never known poverty, hunger or cold. Growing up, a snowy day meant going into the backyard and catching snowflakes, or building a snowman, or sledding with her father. She'd hoped that the beauty of a gentle snowfall would have lightened his mood, but she'd only seemed to have made it worse. She usually wasn't so clumsy with a client's needs. She always prided herself on being able to gauge their weak spots and strengths.

Although she'd planned his program with meticulous care, she'd allowed him to bewitch her to only see the wealthy man with a temper and desire for her. However, she knew she couldn't blame him—she'd let herself see him only one way. As if he were two-dimensional because it kept her heart safe. She didn't want to admire him too much. She didn't want to know all that he'd gone through to get to where he was. How had he learned to fight so well? Had he learned that in prison, or from before? How much had prison affected him? Was she just a challenge to him? They had little in common. He still had too many rough edges. Edges she knew he'd paid her to smooth, but ones that attracted her. But she knew that focusing on only half of his story was being unfair, and it hurt to know that tonight she'd failed him. "Let's go."

Jason didn't argue. He remained silent the rest of the way to her office. When he drove up and parked Abby plastered on a smile, determined that the next outing would be better. "Despite the last hour, it was a good day," she said, desperate to lift the heavy mood in the car. She turned to open the door.

He locked it.

She looked at him, confused, but he stared straight ahead. She unlocked the car.

He locked it again.

She turned to him, annoyed. "Why are you doing that?"

"Don't feel sorry for me."

"What?"

Jason sighed. "I may not have had the perfect childhood, and it may have been rough, but I don't want you pitying me. I don't want you to over-sympathize or try to soften your approach. The one thing I like about you is that you don't take my crap." He turned to her, his dark gaze holding her still. "Don't start now."

"I didn't plan to."

"Good." He unlocked the door. "Besides, there is one bright spot about today."

"What is it?"

"I only have to wait three more weeks." His face split into a naughty grinned, then he winked.

He was still counting down the weeks!
Abby didn't know whether to be frustrated or thrilled.

She wasn't even sure she was making much progress with him. He had been able to manage his temper until they'd run into that horrid man today. But Abby didn't have much hope that he'd be all that different at the end of the next three weeks—despite the online work she had also given him. While she was looking forward to the six weeks ending, she found herself becoming more anxious.

Was she ready to be with him when he was no longer her client?

Chapter 10

"Is this really necessary?" Jason asked while Abby smoothed down the fake mustache and goatee she'd pasted on his face. They sat in her office.

"Yes, I don't want anyone to recognize you." She stepped back and looked at him. "There are two main areas we need to work on. The two important *T*s."

Jason grinned and lazily looked over at her. He was willing to go along with the charade. He enjoyed the time he was spending with her, and loved when he was able to work closely with her.

"And it does not stand for *tits and tail*," Abby said in a dry tone.

"I didn't say anything."

"I told you that your face says it all."

He shrugged. "I'm working on it."

"The two *T*s stand for *tact and temper*. You lack tact and have a horrible temper, which we'll get back to later. Today we'll work on tact. So you're going to spend a day helping women in a boutique."

"Why a women's boutique? Why not a tool shop?"

"Because I want you to feel out of your element, and this clientele expects to be treated at a certain level. You will smile, you will make them feel good and you will listen. And whatever they want, you'll make it happen."

"Let me be a waiter for a day." Although Jason had had no problem entertaining women in order to close business deals, it had always been on his terms.

"No."

"A bouncer?"

"Definitely not. Now, come on."

A half hour later, they arrived at a small boutique. Abby introduced Jason to the store owner, and she gave him some simple instructions before they opened the doors.

One lady came in and picked up a top that was clearly too large and held it up against her.

She looked at Jason. "Do you think this will work?"

"Only if you're buying it for a friend."

She frowned. "I'm shopping for myself."

He picked up another item. "Then this one is better."

"But I like the pattern on this one."

"But you're too—"

"It will be lovely with matching earrings," Abby said, leading the woman away.

Jason stifled a yawn and absently watched another woman stare in the full-length mirror at a pair of jeans she'd just tried on. "Do you think this makes my butt look big?"

"No," Jason said.

She beamed. "Really?"

"Yes, your butt is big, so it doesn't make any difference."

"What?" the woman said, staring at him openmouthed.

"Excuse me," Abby said, rushing forward. "I'm sorry. He's new here. You look great." She said a few more words to soothe the woman's wounded ego, then grabbed Jason's hand and led him outside. Neither of them wore coats, so the shock of the cold day instantly made her shiver, but Jason barely felt anything.

"What is wrong with you?" she demanded.

"Why do you keep asking me that?"

"Because you're driving me insane. Have you listened to nothing I've taught you? You've done the exercises and listened to the lectures, yet you're acting as if you've learned nothing. We're working on tact today. *Tact,* do you know what that means?"

He pulled out his phone. "Do you want my own definition or the one from the dictionary?"

"Put that away and listen. Tact is an art. It is a skill of delicacy. You use your words like a hammer, but instead they should fall like a feather. If someone is trying something on that is not their size, you kindly let them know that 'perhaps' it's unflattering and make another suggestion. If they're adamant, you say nothing. If a woman asks if something makes a certain part of her body look big, you say no."

"But what if it is big and she likes it that way? How am I supposed to know the difference? She's an attractive woman, and she's got a great figure."

"Women rarely want to look bigger than they are. Now, remember to be gentle. Make them feel good. I want you to make a woman smile." Abby opened the door. "Remember, be tactful."

Jason reluctantly went back to his post, counting down the days when he wouldn't have to be subject to this kind of activity again. He watched a woman try on a top that dipped low in the front. "I'm not sure this will work," she said, gazing at the mirror, her hands on her hips. "I'm wearing a new bra. Do you think it gives me enough cleavage?"

"The shirt or the bra?" Jason replied.

The woman frowned. "Both, I guess. I hope it gives me a good lift, makes me look a little bigger," she said with a giggle.

Jason looked at her small chest, not understanding why she was worried about that when she had legs that could make a man's mouth water. Then he remembered Abby's advice and felt safe. He shook his head. "No, I don't think—"

Abby rushed over and quickly covered his mouth. "You look fabulous. You don't have to worry about a thing."

The woman grinned, then disappeared into the changing room. Abby took Jason's hand and again led him outside.

"Why don't you just admit it?" Jason said.

"What?"

He pulled her close. "That you like having me all to yourself."

"I'm trying not to strangle you."

Jason sighed. "What did I do wrong now?"

"You should have said yes."

"You told me to say no. You said that women don't want any parts of their bodies to be bigger than they are."

Abby sighed. "Don't you understand nuance at all?"

"New what?"

"Don't be simple, you know exactly what I mean."

"I told you to put me in a tool store, or even a fast-food joint would be better than this place. What the hell do I know about women's clothes? And why don't they ask straight questions that are easy to answer?"

"Exactly, not all questions are easy to answer. People

don't always say what they really mean. You need to understand body cues, sense how someone else feels."

"Fine, put me behind a bar. I'll listen to drunk people tell me about their lives."

"No, you can do this. The problem is you're taking everything at face value. You need to start reading people. What do most people want? To be treated well, respected, to feel good. We're not leaving here until you make a woman smile."

"And if I don't?"

"We're coming back tomorrow." Abby opened the door, and said with the command of a drill sergeant, "Now, go."

Jason went back inside and inwardly swore. It wasn't as if he wasn't trying. He really was. He just couldn't read people. He'd never taken the time. Abby was right, he never paid attention. He was good with his mother and animals, but people he didn't know, that was harder for him. Growing up on the streets of Baltimore, Jason knew that caring too much made you a victim. It was eat or be eaten. He couldn't assert himself that way here.

Tact. She wanted him to be tactful. He saw a woman come out of the dressing room wearing a dress meant for a much younger person. She had the figure, but the dress didn't suit her.

"I have a hot date tonight," she said.

Jason just grinned. It was best he didn't say anything.

"What do you think?"

"That you're a very attractive woman." *Wearing the wrong dress,* he silently added.

"You do?"

He nodded.

"I hope he feels the same. I haven't dated in a long time, since my husband died."

He nodded. Were women really this chatty while buying clothes?

"I want to give the right impression. I don't want him to think I'm too easy."

Jason knew that her date would take one look at the outfit and have her undressed by the end of the evening. She screamed desperation. He could tell that she was a woman of class, but she thought she had to compete with young women for attention. "You're wearing the wrong dress," he said, then saw Abby wince and the woman look confused. "For a woman of your obvious taste. Um…this is a third-date dress. A first-date dress should be something that makes you feel comfortable and makes the man wonder what's next." He grabbed another outfit. "Something like this."

"Wouldn't that make me look old?"

"No, you'll make it look young. You're a very beautiful woman. If you want this date to focus on your body and undress you with his eyes all night, then buy the first dress. If you want him to focus on you, then wear the second one."

She grinned. "I'll get them both."

"Then, he's a lucky man. She'll ring you up at the counter."

"Thank you."

Jason resisted pumping his fist in the air. Success! He'd gotten the woman to smile. Now he could leave.

"What do you think this outfit says?" a full-figured young woman asked. She had a cute face, but the dress strained against her body.

That you're in the wrong store. None of the clothes looked her size. "If you feel good, it says all that you want it to."

She giggled, then disappeared in the changing room.

"Do these earrings say—"

"Excuse me." He didn't care what they said or did. He wanted to get out of there. He'd been able to make one woman smile and another woman giggle, but he wasn't sure how long his lucky streak would last. He went up to Abby. "Let's go."

"You're a hit."

"I don't care. You said we could leave after I made a woman smile."

"Why leave when you're on a roll? You did great."

"I just remembered what I heard a guy say on TV. I still don't know what women are talking about."

"The key is you were listening to them and connecting with them on a different level. A human level. You knew she wanted to make a good impression, and you kindly gave her advice without judging her."

"And this will help me, how?"

"If someone in your office says something ridiculous, don't just focus on what was said, but the intention behind it and the way it was said. So your next assignment is to do something nice for one of your employees."

"Like what?"

"I'm sure you'll think of something."

Two days later, Benny stood in front of Jason's desk looking confused. "Are you sure?"

"Of course I'm sure," Jason said. He wasn't used to being asked that question. Nor was he used to Benny looking uncertain about something. "I'm always sure."

Benny hesitated. "I understand how you may feel, but this is the office."

"I know. Just do what I told you, okay?"

Benny cleared his throat and lowered his voice. "But then everyone will know."

"That's the point."

"Is there something you want to tell me?"

Jason sighed. He wasn't ready to tell Benny that he was doing this to complete an assignment. He knew that his request was out of character, but he wanted to do something nice for the office manager, and he thought this idea was the best he could come up with. "No. I'm trying to be a nicer employer."

Benny nodded. "That's commendable, but—"

"Just do it," Jason said, no longer in the mood to discuss it.

Benny nodded again. "Okay," he said, drawing out the word as if Jason had just made a huge mistake.

Chapter 11

"You. Did. What?"

Jason stared at Abby, not understanding why she didn't look pleased. She actually looked stunned. He'd been looking forward to seeing her again, having her praise him for doing a great job. Instead her eyes had gotten wide, and she'd looked at him as if he'd fallen from another planet. "What did I do wrong? I did what you said."

Abby threw up her hands, then began pacing his living room. "I can't believe this."

"What's wrong with sending the office manager a dozen red roses for her birthday? You told me to do something nice for one of my employees."

Abby stopped pacing and stared at him. "Not with *red* roses! You don't send red roses. Especially to a female."

Jason frowned. "It's better to send it a man?"

"No." Abby sat down in front of Jason and clasped her hands together. She took a deep breath, then said slowly, "You just have broken a key business etiquette rule."

"I thought women like flowers."

"They do, but you're sending the wrong message. You

should have sent her daisies. Or if you had to go with roses, which is dangerous, you should have made sure that they were yellow. Yellow is a symbol of friendship at least, but red symbolizes romantic interest."

"Oh." Jason thought for a moment, now understanding Benny's hesitation. He swore. "That's why she kept grinning at me all day."

Abby held out her hand. "She wasn't angry?"

Jason pulled out his wallet and handed her a bill. "No."

Abby covered her eyes and lowered her head. "Oh, no, that's even worse."

"Why? At least I know she liked them."

Abby looked up at him with pity. "It also means she likes you. And she thinks you like her—a lot. You'll have to clear things up with her, or it will be awkward. Take all the blame and let her down easy."

"And how do you suggest I do that? Do I tell her it was a mistake?"

"Not like that, but you speak to her in private."

"If I talk to her in private, won't she get the wrong idea?"

"She already has the wrong idea. However, you can't embarrass her. You'll talk to her in private and say that you hope she liked the flowers, but that you realized it was inappropriate to choose red roses since she is a colleague and you respect her as a professional. Something like that."

Jason stretched an arm the length of the couch. He'd get Benny to handle it. He'd call him the moment Abby was gone. "So, are you ready to give up?"

"Give up?"

"Yes, on me. Am I a hopeless case?"

"No one is a hopeless case. You're a little more tactful. I think we're making excellent progress."

"We only have one more session after this."

"I know. Take me to your bedroom."

Jason froze. "Don't say things like that unless you mean it."

Abby stood and grinned. "I do mean it. I want to see what's in your closet."

Jason stood and narrowed his eyes. "You've got a mean streak."

"Sorry, I couldn't help myself. I wanted to see your face." She turned toward the hall. "Lead the way."

"Why do you want to see my closet?"

She pointed to his wrist. "You have money. Why do you wear a watch with a cloth band? That does not give a professional appearance. It's best to go with a metal or leather band in the standard colors of black or brown. Brown leather will be a nice accent with belts and shoes. And a tie should reach the top of your belt buckle, while socks should be long enough to reach the calf."

Jason yawned. "Am I really supposed to care?"

"Plus, you seem to wear only one color. I want to see what other options you have. You have to look your best at the Madison Ball. Let's go."

The moment Abby opened his closet, she quickly looked through the selection then said, "We need to do some shopping."

"On one condition," Jason said with a mysterious grin.

"What?"

Chapter 12

Abby stared at Jason, unsure. "You want me to be your date?"

"Yes."

It was a strange request. She'd never had a client ask her to attend a function with them before, as their date. At times she would attend different events and stay back and observe, but never up close. And being close to Jason was a dangerous proposition. She didn't trust her judgment in men. She didn't trust their agendas. All the men she'd fallen for had used her.

It had started in high school when one boyfriend only liked her because she did his homework. Another boyfriend she'd helped become president of the student council, and then he dropped her. Then she'd met Charles, and she knew the outcome of that. Jason wanted to remake his image and just have a little fun on the side. Once he was finished with her, he'd go on to the next woman. She wasn't going to get hurt again. She'd take his money and nothing else. She decided this would be the last time she'd see him.

To her annoyance, her heart still leaped whenever she

saw him, and she tried not to picture him naked, or re-member how the touch of his lips felt on hers. She was a professional, and soon they'd never know each other. Plus, anytime her mind wandered too far, she remembered her bet with Judith and all that was at stake.

Thankfully, there had been some progress. He was more subdued. He was less on edge. He still didn't smile much, although she'd tried on a number of occasions to get him to. He didn't do chitchat, he still didn't like suits, and al-though she'd hinted at adding some colors to his wardrobe, he'd ignored the suggestion. But he seemed more relaxed, less in a hurry. More genial somehow, and vulnerable. He'd hinted at how hard it had been to rebuild after his false conviction. Now, he seemed more human somehow, and she wanted to see him succeed, not just for herself but for him, too. She couldn't take credit for his transformation, although she would, so that Judith would pay her rent for the next six months. And she hoped, with his success, that he would refer other high-paying clients to her.

"I'm sure you wouldn't have any trouble getting a date. You don't need me."

"That's not true."

"You can't get a date?"

"Not the right one. I need a woman who doesn't cling and doesn't tremble."

"Is that supposed to make sense?"

"The first type of woman I attract is the type who likes to hang on to me. They like to watch me and be with me all the time. They cling. The other type find me interesting. An experience they can put on their bucket list. But they're nervous around me. If I send them a look, they shake. You're neither of those types, and I find that refreshing."

"You could go alone."

"I don't want to."

"How important is this party? What's your agenda?"

"Two key people I'd eventually like to partner with will be there. One owns a small manufacturing company that makes specialized equipment. I really want to work with him to help design several rides that accommodate people with limitations and disabilities, but still give them a time of their life. The other individual is president of a major medical supply company. If I get to work with him, I'll be able to get access to medical supplies and equipment way below wholesale price, and be able to pass the savings on to individuals who visit my resorts and need medical attention. I really want my resort to…"

That's when Jason told Abby all about his idea for his resorts and how he'd turn them into vacation getaways for adults with disabilities and life-threatening illnesses, and also for families healing from grief.

Abby loved the idea of his vision but knew that, although he'd made significant changes, his past reputation could still get in the way. "Why didn't you tell me this before? I thought you just wanted to make money and prove that you were a big man. This changes everything."

"It does?"

"You're a big softy underneath."

He frowned, offended. "I'm not a softy. I still want to make a profit and—"

She shook her head. "Sorry, I used the wrong word. I meant that you have a big heart. People like that, and it will work in your favor." She clapped her hands together. "Okay, I'll go to the cocktail party with you. But you'll have to wear a suit."

His lip curled. "No, I don't."

"If you want me to come, you will."

"Suits don't fit me."

"You're wealthy enough to have them custom-made."

"I know that, it's just—"

"I'll help you. Trust me."

Jason sighed. "Okay."

That day, they made an appointment to get together for a fitting, and then she left. Back in her office, Abby did a little dance. She was finally going to get him in a suit! And she'd get to spend more time with him. She looked forward to that.

"You're in a good mood," Judith said in a dour tone, standing in the doorway.

Abby stopped and composed herself. She smoothed down her hair and lifted her chin. "Did you want something?"

"How is it working with the gorilla?"

"Don't call him that."

"You're right—he's better looking, but still scary." She folded her arms. "But you don't look scared at all."

"I'm not. I'm making great progress."

"You still have a week left. Anything can happen."

"He's changed. You'll see."

"He hasn't been out in public much."

"He's attending the Madison Ball, and I'll be there."

Judith raised her eyebrows, amazed. "How did you get invited?"

"I'm going as his—"

"Escort?"

"Date," Abby corrected. "This is purely business."

"It never is with a man like that. He's got a hidden agenda. I'd watch out."

"Like most people, you're wrong about him. Be prepared to be amazed."

She was going to lose. Judith paced her living room. The house stood quiet. Her two kids were asleep, and her husband was away on a business trip. But she couldn't rest. She was afraid that if she closed her eyes, she'd have nightmares. Nightmares of Abby winning and telling her she had to pay for the office. Why had Abby forced her to make such a ridiculous bet? If Abby hadn't found out that she'd been skimming some of her clients, she wouldn't be in this mess. It wasn't as if she'd really hurt anyone.

It wasn't fair. Abby wasn't supposed to win. *She was.* She thought she'd had everything set. Jason Ward was a known disaster. How could Abby handle him so well? It would be a professional humiliation, as well. Why hadn't Jason given Abby sleepless nights and stomachaches like Judith had with that awful client? Why did they seem to have a relationship that defied words? Sometimes Jason would look at Abby without saying anything, and she'd understand. It didn't make sense. He was all wrong. He was supposed to make Abby lose. What was she going to do? She couldn't lose. Abby had looked so happy and smug. She was always smug, even in school when she'd had no right to be.

She had to find Jason's soft spot, and she knew exactly who to go to.

Chapter 13

Damn, he should have known she'd make him wear a suit. He should have thought of taking her somewhere else instead of to the stupid Madison Ball, but it was an important event and there would be key people there who had nothing to do with his past. Jason stared at himself in the mirror. He thought he could live the rest of his life without having to wear a suit again. It had certainly been a goal while he was growing up. His mother had always insisted on putting him in suits.

"A man in a suit gets respect," she liked to say. "And make sure your shoes shine." He swore. He remembered his dress shoes. Every Saturday he'd had his shoe polish and cloth and had to make his shoes shine until her face could be seen in the reflection. But he wasn't a kid anymore, and if Abby wanted him in a suit, he'd wear one. He just hoped she wouldn't make a habit out of it.

"No," Abby said, standing behind him, using the same stool the tailor had. He saw her frown reflected in the full-length mirror. Being close to her and unable to touch her had been difficult. He had to use all his willpower not to lean against her.

"This is the third one I've tried on. I told you—"

"We've only just started. Be patient."

"I'm quitting after the fifth."

Abby rested her hands on his shoulders. "Think of all the people you'll make happy if you're able to partner with those companies and make your resort one of a kind."

He sighed. Right now, with her breath against his ear, he could only think of her lips and her naked body wrapped around him. "Hmm."

They finally settled on the eighth suit. The selection even surprised Jason, who'd never felt comfortable, no matter what he selected. Abby had been able to give the tailor great instructions, and the adjustments that were made to the suit surprised him, although initially he had been skeptical. No double-breasted jacket, just a slim, fitted one with room for him to move; the pleat at the back was made just a little longer to accommodate his size, and the shoulder width widened. Jason watched Abby talk to the tailor, giving him some final instructions, and wondered what he could do to treat her.

Abby couldn't remember the last time she'd had such fun shopping. Finding the right suit had been a great challenge, and she'd been able to convince Jason to place an order for two suits rather than one. He'd also placed an order for three customized dress shirts in pastel green, blue and lavender. The colors made his mocha-brown skin look delectable. She had to control her desire not to want to eat off him.

Next they went shopping for a new watch. Abby knew that Jason wasn't someone she could get to wear any kind of jewelry, but he needed something to go with his new wardrobe, and a handsome watch was her next bet, along with one or two lapel pins, which Jason loudly objected to.

"What do I need with a lapel button?"

"They can be great conversation starters."

"I'll look like a…"

"A man of interest." She ignored whatever he had to say, and selected two twenty-four karat gold lapel pins, one in the shape of a heart, the other a wishbone.

As they walked to another part of the mall, Abby stopped when she saw a gorgeous red dress displayed in one of the specialty shop windows. She sighed, wistful.

"Do you want it?" Jason asked her, stopping in front of the shop.

"Someday."

"How about today?"

"But—"

"You want me to look good, and I want the same for you."

Abby bit her lip.

Jason opened the door to the store and pulled Abby inside, then called over one of the attendants. "We would like to try on that dress." He pointed to the dress in the window, then gave Abby's dress size. Abby stood, speechless. She hadn't told him her size. She was surprised to know he'd taken notice of what it was.

She tried it on and loved it. Over the next forty minutes, Abby felt as if she was in Cinderella's castle as she got the dress fitted. It had been a long time since she had splurged on anything for herself. The dressmaker, a busy woman, spent time making any final adjustments, to ensure the dress fit Abby perfectly. "This dress looks like it was made just for you, my dear."

Abby caught Jason's gaze in the mirror, and she could imagine his thoughts as his gaze followed how the fabric fell smoothly around her form, emphasizing her curves. The neckline provided enough view of her cleavage, without being too obvious, and she could imagine him holding her right now, caressing her skin, burying his face between her breasts and...

"So, what do you think?" the attendant asked her suddenly, unceremoniously jerking her out of her daydream.

"It's perfect!" Abby said in a too high tone. She cleared her throat when she saw Jason grin. "I mean, I like it."

"You'll need shoes to go with the dress, right?" Jason asked after he'd paid.

Abby's heart stopped. She could have kissed him. "You know how to seduce a woman."

Jason caught her expression and grinned. "This is just a taste of things to come."

Instead of feeling annoyed, Abby felt aroused, excited. She could get used to this luxury again—fine dining, trips abroad, shopping sprees. She certainly could get used to him. The fact that he made her heart race, made her skin tingle, didn't frighten her anymore. She didn't mind that he made grand faux pas, that he could still be tactless and still had to work on his temper. She liked him and felt most herself with him. While she worked on his flaws, he exposed some of hers as well and didn't judge her. She had to stop making business an excuse and state what she wanted—and what she wanted was to be with Jason Ward.

Abby selected a pair of evening shoes and then a small clutch purse. It had been so long since she'd been able to shop this freely, to spend without worrying about the price tag. She felt as if she were in a dream or reuniting with old friends. She looked at labels she'd only had a passing acquaintance with, and now could know more intimately. At the cash register, Abby tried to keep her face composed to prepare herself for the bill, but she never got to see it. Jason handed the clerk his credit card, and she rang the items up.

The store clerk helped them with the bags, and Jason gave the young man a tip.

Abby watched him close the trunk. "Jason—"

"Don't ask me how much or how you can pay me back," he said, walking to the driver's side.

"I wasn't going to. I'm surprised you stayed around. It must have been boring."

"You looked like you were having fun."

"I was. It was one of the best days I've had in a long time. Thank you."

He rested his arms on the hood of the car and grinned at her. "You don't have to say it. You can show me."

"How?"

"Think of something," he said, then disappeared inside the car.

Abby sat inside the car and put on her seat belt, the car suddenly feeling smaller and more intimate than before. Two kisses had passed between them. Did he expect a third? When they had been in the store and he had mentioned buying shoes to match her dress, she could have thrown her arms around him and kissed him. But if she'd kissed him, he would have made her forget about shoes altogether. Suddenly she was aware of how the intoxicating scent of him—whether it was his cologne or soap, she still didn't know—lingered in the air. She'd wait until after the cocktail party before she told him how she felt.

He drove her to her town house and carried her bags to the front door. "Thanks again," she said, annoyed that her hand shook when she placed the key in the lock.

"I'm hungry."

She lifted a brow. "Is that supposed to be some sort of come-on?"

"No, it's a statement of fact. I'm hungry. Aren't you?"

"Are you inviting yourself inside?"

"Only if I don't get an invitation." He held up her bags. "Don't you think I deserve something to eat?"

"We could have picked something up on our way here," she said, feeling a little guilty. She hadn't realized they'd been out all day. When it came to shopping, the phrase "shop 'til you drop" suited her. She'd totally forgotten about food. She softened. She couldn't blame him for being hungry, and he was right, especially with all the things he had bought for her.

"We can still order in."

Abby sighed. "Fine, come in." She opened the door, then abruptly stopped and spun around to him. "But no comments about my place."

He nodded. But when he stepped inside, he gave a low whistle. "You've got to be kidding."

Boxes filled her entire living room. "I told you not to make a comment."

Jason set her bags down. "What is all this stuff?"

"We just had a clothing drive for the babies at the hospital, and they needed a place to put things."

"And they couldn't find a storage space?"

"My place is cheaper."

"And smaller."

"It's a decent-sized place," Abby said, offended. "It only looks small because of all the boxes."

"How long do they need to be here?"

"Just a couple more months, then we'll ship them to the different centers."

"Hmm. After lunch we'll look at storage spaces."

"I already told you that's not—"

"I'll pay. Deduct it from my bill. I can't have you getting taken advantage of."

"No one is taking advantage of me."

"Where would this stuff go if you weren't here?"

"I don't know."

"Exactly. I guarantee you they'd find a place." Before she could say more, Jason headed into the kitchen. "Okay, what's for lunch?" He opened the fridge, then stopped. "No wonder you're so skinny. There's nothing in here."

"I haven't been shopping. I wasn't expecting anyone."

He narrowed his eyes. "You're not telling me something." He rested against the counter. "I knew your business was bad, but it's worse than I thought, isn't it?"

Abby stared at him, stunned. "What do you mean? How can you think that?"

He pointed. "Those items over there are probably set aside for a donation, but those other items—" he pointed to a pile of carefully stacked clothing "—are varied and makes me wonder if you sell items online to supplement your income."

"I'm good." Abby shook her head, annoyed. "No, great at what I do, but it takes time to grow a business. And do you know how difficult it is to have a sister like Judith around who steals clients from you or sabotages you?"

"No." He paused. "Wait, did you say sister?"

"Yes, my little sister who always has to do what I do. Of all the careers she could have gone into, she chose one similar to mine. She decided to work with a woman whom I'd considered a mentor, and in the same building I do. You'd think it would be enough that she's Mom's favorite, and she's got the house, the husband and the kids, but she still has to compete with me in everything. And don't let her fool you into thinking she does it because she somehow admires me. That's not it. She just likes trying to destroy anything that's mine. But that's way too much information for you to know about me, so why don't you just leave?" Abby didn't want to bore him with the real truth.

The truth was that their parents had been unable to have

children and had adopted her as a baby, when they were both in their early forties. Then three years later, surprise, they had Judith. Their miracle baby. Although her parents tried their best to treat them equally, Judith always felt as if they preferred Abby over her because they'd chosen her while she'd just been a surprise.

It was a jealousy that consumed her. She wanted to go everywhere Abby went, and whenever her parents bought something for Abby, they had to buy the exact same item for Judith, or she would throw a fit, saying they didn't love her as much. All the while reminding Abby, every chance she got, that her real parents hadn't wanted her. Her up-bringing had left a wound that Abby's adopted parents hadn't completely healed with their sometimes preferential treatment of Judith.

So she wasn't surprised by her sister's behavior stealing her clients, and her bet that she wouldn't be able to make over Jason Ward in six weeks. But she would prove to her that she deserved to be part of the family.

"I'm sure she's not your mother's favorite," Jason said. "We sometimes—"

"Mom told me so," Abby said, even though that wasn't completely true. Her mother had really said that Judith was insecure and needed her more.

"Oh." He started to grin. "Make sure to wear one of your new outfits to work." In addition to the red dress, he had allowed her to indulge a bit and had added several select items to her shopping bag.

Abby giggled. "Her skin will turn green."

"Do you need more referrals?"

"I plan to make you one of my biggest success stories, then people will come running." Abby didn't want to appear desperate. She believed her client list would grow exponentially once she succeeded with Jason.

"Let's eat."

They ordered some Thai food, and after they'd finished eating, he helped her pack up some of the items.

"What's this?" He pointed to a box filled with baby dummies.

"They're used for CPR practice. We provide them to community centers to help with their first aid training."

Jason lifted up one of the dummies with interest. "How do you do CPR on a baby?"

"Like this." Abby got down on the floor and showed him how to perform CPR, and also showed him what to do with a choking victim. To her surprise, he took to it like a pro.

"Hope I never have to use either method," Jason said once he'd finished.

"Me neither," Abby said, packing up the box. "But it's good to know." Then she looked at the bags again. "I got more items than you did."

"You have a bigger challenge."

"Challenge?"

"Yes, to make me look good."

But he canceled their last appointment. Abby sat in her office and stared at her phone, concerned.

"You might as well pay up now," Judith said, walking into her office. "He's not coming, is he?"

"He had an emergency."

"That's the easiest lie to use."

Jason didn't lie. He wouldn't have canceled without a good reason. Something was wrong, but he'd been deliberately vague. She called him back, but he wouldn't answer. She texted him and still got no answer. She called Henry.

"Has something happened to Jason?"

"No, it's…it's his mother. She's in the hospital."

"Oh, no, what happened?"

"We don't know yet. She felt dizzy and had to be taken in. That's all I can say."

"Which hospital?" she asked, but he'd hung up before she could get an answer. She called again, but her message went directly to his voice mail. Abby hung up, knowing she had to see Jason.

"Where are you going?" Judith asked, watching Abby grab her coat.

"Out," Abby said, then left. She drove to his place.

"Mr. Ward isn't here," his butler said, when he answered the door.

"I know, that's why I'm here. I can't reach him."

"He's at the hospital."

"Which one?"

He hesitated, then opened the door wider. "Why don't you come in and sit down?"

"Just tell me where he is."

He shook his head. "He doesn't like to be disturbed."

Abby sighed. The butler was right. If something was wrong, she didn't have the right to barge in and demand answers. "Tell him to call me when he gets back."

"It's a long drive back. At least have a refreshment before you leave." He held out a tray filled with an assortment of energy bars.

"Thanks, I'll have just one."

She didn't, though. She couldn't eat anything. She couldn't rest and decided to look around. Then she saw his Olympic-size indoor pool and knew what she could do to calm her nerves before he returned. She knew she was taking a risk, but she needed to do something, and she'd make it quick. She always had her swimming gear in the trunk of her car. Abby went out to her car, grabbed her bag, changed into a swimsuit, then dove in.

* * *

The beast was back. Jason hung up his coat and swore. The doctor said they'd caught the cancer in time, but that didn't make Jason feel any better. There would be another set of treatments, and he didn't want his mother to have to go through that again.

"You have a visitor," his butler said.

"What?"

"Yes, Ms. Baylor. She said she called you."

Jason looked at his phone and saw the messages and texts. He'd turned his phone off. He wondered if Abby would believe why he had to cancel. "Where is she?"

"In the pool."

Jason glanced at his watch. "This late?"

His butler shrugged. "That's where she is."

Jason walked to the pool. Seeing Abby in a swimsuit would certainly take his mind off things. He walked into the enclosed room and spotted Abby under the water, at the bottom of the pool—not moving. Why wasn't she moving? His heart raced as a series of fears flooded his mind. He thought of possibly losing his mother to cancer, and how he'd lost Gwen. And for a second, that's who he saw—Gwen unmoving. He tore off his jacket and jumped in. He dove to the bottom and grabbed her, then pulled her to the surface.

"Jason!" Abby sputtered. "What are you doing?"

He couldn't think or talk. All that mattered was that she was alive. She was all right. But he still couldn't let her go. He lifted her out of the water, then pulled himself out, as well.

"Jason? My goodness, you're soaked. You didn't even change your clothes."

He breathed so hard, his chest ached, not from exertion,

but from fear. A fear he hadn't felt in years. "I thought…I thought you were drowning. You weren't moving."

"I was holding my breath."

Jason wiped water from his face and stood. *She's alive. Thank goodness she's alive.* He didn't care how angry she got. He stumbled to the door. "I'm sorry."

"Jason." Abby took his hand. "Come on, you need to go change."

"I'll be fine after a drink."

Dripping wet, Jason went into the sitting room, poured himself a drink and took a long swallow. Now that the imaginary crisis was over, he felt like an idiot. He'd panicked. He hadn't done that since he was a young man.

"You really should change," Abby said, draping a towel around his shoulders. "You could slip and fall."

He didn't move. "I'm sorry I scared you," he said in an anguished voice, not sure if he was saying it to Abby or the ghost he'd just seen. He looked at Abby's face, ashamed he could have frightened her in any way.

She gently tugged his arm. "I'm all right." She hesitated. "What's wrong?"

He wished he could put his thoughts into words. Everything was wrong. "I'm sorry," he said again, then covered her mouth with his.

Chapter 14

Abby remembered feeling the pounding of his heart, then the sensation of his soft lips on hers. Satisfying her desire, but leaving her with more questions. Why had he jumped in after her, and why did he keep apologizing? What was the note of anguish in his tone? What did it mean? But she would let those questions wait. She removed his wet shirt. He removed the strap of her swimsuit.

"Wait," she said.

"Why?"

"I should go first. I have a lot more to remove than you do."

"Then you need to hurry up," Jason said, removing the other strap.

She unbuttoned his shirt. "Are you always this impatient?"

"No. Once I have you naked, I plan to take my time."

She unzipped his jeans. "I don't believe you."

"When this is over, you will." He slid off her swimsuit, his hands hot against her skin. Soon his warm, wet flesh lay over hers. She arched into him. He buried his face in her neck, his breath hot against her skin when he spoke. "Beautiful."

"I didn't bring anything," she whispered.

"I didn't expect you to."

"I mean, I didn't expect for this to happen."

"The moment I saw you, this is all I've thought about."

Abby shook her head. "Jason, that's not what I mean."

He frowned. "Then what is it?"

She glanced down below his waist, then met his eyes again. "I'm ready to make his acquaintance, but not without an escort."

Jason's frown increased. "Is this some sort of riddle?"

Abby wrapped her hand around his penis. "I don't mind just using my hand if you want, until we can do this another time."

He groaned. "Don't keep doing that. I don't want to come unless I'm inside you."

"But that can't be."

"Why not?"

"You really don't know what I'm talking about?"

Jason closed his eyes and grit his teeth. "I can barely put words together when you're holding me like that, let alone follow this conversation."

"Do you have condoms?"

"Why didn't you just say that before?"

"I was trying to be delicate."

Jason sent a significant glance at her hand, and the corner of his mouth kicked up in a grin. "You call that being delicate?"

She let him go. "You weren't getting the hint."

"If you expect me to think, don't distract me like that." He stood and went to a panel in the wall.

"What are you doing?" she asked.

"Calling to get me some condoms."

Abby rushed over and grabbed his hand. "You can't do that!"

"Why not?"

"Because we're naked."

"I'll open the door a crack. I'll make sure he doesn't see you."

"It's not right."

"What's not right about it? I'll tell him to bring a towel, too, if you want?"

"No, then he'll know what we're doing."

"Relax, I pay him well to be discreet."

"Can't we just go to your room?"

He sighed. "Okay, you wait here." Before she could stop him, he left the room.

Abby squeezed her eyes closed. She couldn't believe he'd left the room totally naked. If his staff wondered what he was doing before, they wouldn't wonder now. But it was his house, and he had the right to do whatever he wanted. Abby looked around the room. Suddenly, darkness descended. She couldn't understand why. There was no sign of a storm. She didn't know whether to stay still or cry out. She decided to stay still; she didn't want to draw attention to herself. She had made herself comfortable on the small couch. The fireplace came alive with a blazing fire, and she heard the door creek open and saw a single candle in the doorway. Then she noticed Jason wearing a mask and cape.

"I thought you were going to put only one thing on."

"I thought this would be a lot more fun." He sat down on the couch, setting the candle aside. "You look cold," he said, drawing the cape around her.

She shivered.

"Don't be scared."

"I'm not."

It was only when he came back that she realized how much she'd missed him, how much she wanted this. One hand slid down her stomach to the curve of her hip. His mouth covered one breast, his tongue teasing her nipple.

A sensory overload of pleasure hit her. The light of the dancing flames reflected on the ceiling seemed to mirror the inferno inside her. An inferno only he could extinguish. She writhed beneath him with an urgent persuasion.

He groaned. "If you keep moving like that, I won't be able to take my time."

"Exactly, I don't want you to." She took off his mask. "We can play games another time. Right now, I want you." She teased the tip of him with the center of her. "Right here."

Jason didn't need any more encouragement. Soon their bodies melted into one in a fiery explosion of passion that made them both tremble. Abby felt her entire body shudder with a shimmering ecstasy that made her feel as if she could float. She knew it would feel good, she knew that he would feel right, but what she didn't know was that he was the man she'd been waiting for all her life. No other man had ever made her feel this way. His cape made her at first think of a vampire, but she knew instead that he was a magician—she was powerless under his spell. She could teach him manners and smooth his rough edges, but here he was the teacher, and she was ready to learn every lesson.

Passion. She'd never felt such passion; he made her feel uninhibited, unashamed. Free. He'd ripped away the tightly wound control that she'd wrapped herself in. She would emerge a new woman.

Jason already knew he was a new man as he held a wildcat in his arms. He had no desire to train her; he liked her soft scratches, the wet feel of her tongue on his chest, how she tightened around him, inviting him deeper inside a place he'd never grow tired of. This was his redemption. But he was concerned that he'd revealed too much of himself, and he'd fix that.

As they lay on the rug in front of the fire, Abby rested a hand on his chest. "Your heart is still racing."

He covered her hand with his. "I can't help it."

"It was racing when you pulled me out of the water, too."

His hand fell to his lap. "I'm so sorry."

"You don't have to apologize. Just explain."

"Gwen," he said in a soft voice.

"What?"

"My first love. She died, and I couldn't save her." He shook his head and swallowed. "I couldn't do anything."

"Jason, you can't torture yourself."

His eyes met hers. *I thought you had died, and I can't lose you,* he'd meant to say, but kissed her instead. He hadn't meant to reveal that many regrets. He didn't want her pity. He didn't want her to see how different their lives had been. He wanted her to see him as the man he was now, not the boy he had been. He hated sharing his inadequacy. How much he had failed Gwen. It was dangerous how easily Abby was able to slip through his defenses. But he wouldn't let that happen again. He was Jason Ward, a success, and he'd make sure that was the only Jason she saw. He drew away and cupped her face. "I wasn't thinking clearly after seeing my mother in the hospital."

"How is she? What happened?"

"She had a dizzy spell. She's fine now. But she faces another round of chemo."

"I'm sorry to hear that."

"Does that mean I can finally take you out on a date?"

"You missed your last appointment."

"I'll make it up."

"After the charity ball, we'll discuss dinner."

He grinned.

"What's that grin for?"

He gathered her close. "I'm thinking of a lot more than dinner."

The music pulsated around her, and Judith could feel the rhythm rock through her body. She also felt a pair of eyes on her. Judith let her body move slow and easy to the music, then she felt his breath on her neck. His arm wrapped around her waist and claimed her, as if she were his prize for the evening. She didn't mind. She knew who he was, and obviously he knew who she was.

"So, what's making you so hot tonight?" he asked, nuzzling his mouth against her neck. He was hot, and a little dangerous, just the way she liked them.

"I think I've got some news you can use." She moved her body closer to his. They were in perfect harmony. Judith had met Dennis Collins one night at the Atrium, a high-class nightclub she liked to frequent without her husband, Stephen. She loved her husband, had a good marriage and lived a secure life, but at times she needed an outlet for her wilder side. Stephen didn't mind; besides, she always told him she needed time to spend with her girlfriends.

But she had another reason for coming tonight. She knew Dennis had been Jason's former business partner, and wanted to cause a little trouble for Abby. Abby had looked a little too happy after she'd proudly told her that she'd rescheduled her final appointment with Jason.

"If you've got something good, it could be worth your while."

"Your former business partner and a friend of mine seem to have something on you," she teased.

"What are you talking about?"

"I overheard her talking to Jason about information he had gotten from the lawyer he'd worked with. You know, the one who helped get his conviction overturned." She moved in closer, their bodies entwined, but still in time with the music. "I think Abby found out something about a certain someone having information they may be able to use to help recoup some of Jason's financial losses. Abby and Jason have really hit it off. Hell, you'd think they were a real couple the way they carry on. He's really into her." Judith felt her jealousy rise, but knew she needed to remain civil. "I mean, they even went shopping together. Now, I understand image makeover, professional and personal. I mean, it's what I do, but what's going on between those two seems to be more. He keeps buying her things."

"What do you mean this Abby woman has information?"

"I don't know exactly what she knows, but I overheard them talking about going public with the information they have and Jason getting back what was his. They've been busy getting ready to attend the Madison Ball, and I think that's where they plan to make this announcement."

"So, when is this event happening and where?"

Judith told him, then left, satisfied that she'd set the stage. Abby thought she was all that, but now Dennis would turn up, make a big scene and ruin everything.

How much did she know? What did she know? How had she found out? How could someone know about the information he had planted? Jason wouldn't try to go after SENTEL again—or would he? He had to make sure. Dennis barely remembered the past several hours as the same questions kept playing over and over in his mind. How much of a threat was Abby Baylor to him?

"You're not paying attention to me tonight. What's on your mind?" the woman beside him softly purred.

Dennis didn't move. He had to think. "We may have some trouble."

She lazily trailed her finger up his thigh. "My husband's out of town. What are you talking about?"

"Ward."

Her finger paused. "Ward stopped being trouble a long time ago."

Dennis shook his head and sat up. "It's not just him. He's been seeing some sort of business consultant, who has begun to get a little nosy."

"We've covered all our tracks. There's no way anyone can come after us."

But Dennis wasn't so sure. Stephanie Armstrong had the protection and power of her husband, and he had no one. Nothing new there; nothing had changed. Her hands always stayed clean, no matter how dirty they were. She had enjoyed burying Jason's reputation with her filthy lie about the so-called assault. The night after Jason had given her the number to the escort service, which had made her furious, Dennis knew she'd make him pay. He knew that for all she said about Jason, that was not the man he knew. He could have any woman he wanted, but her dark tale suited him fine and fit in perfectly with his plan to be rid of Jason. Now he had to make sure *he* wasn't still at risk.

He probably should have stopped sleeping with her years ago, but she'd become a habit he'd been reluctant to quit. Plus, she knew his secrets, and he liked to keep her happy. Having her as an enemy would be a dangerous thing. At least the business was doing well. Not as well as when Jason had been onboard, but Dennis just relegated the slow market to the recession, instead of letting others know it may have something to do with his management. He was the brains. He was the one who'd made the company a success.

Jason had become a liability. He'd had to go. Dennis had never felt a moment's guilt for his actions. He'd done what he'd had to, to save the company—at least that's what he'd convinced himself of. It had been easy to make certain documents go missing and others suddenly appear. But a woman like Abby wouldn't understand his noble sacrifice. He didn't like having to send a former friend to prison, but business was war, and sometimes there were causalities.

Dennis stood and grabbed his pants.

Stephanie sighed with annoyance. "What are you doing?" She stretched out her arm to him. "Come back to bed."

She had the melodic voice of a Siren, and for a moment Dennis considered her request. She could make him forget his troubles. Her soft brown body draped in red silk sheets could help rid him of all the demons in his mind. But he wouldn't let himself succumb. Not tonight. He knew there would be other nights. There always were. "I need to go." Dennis looked under the bed for where he'd tossed his socks, then paused when he noticed something. He saw a man's G-string. He didn't wear a G-string. He picked it up and held it out to her. "What's this?"

Stephanie yawned. "Just put it over there," she said, gesturing vaguely to a corner. "I'll have to tell the maid to do a better job, or she's gone."

"That's not my question, and you know it."

"Don't make a big deal of this. Come back to bed. We can discuss it later."

"We'll discuss it now."

Stephanie raised a brow, looking bored and disappointed. "You didn't think you were the only one, did you?" He knew her overly conservative husband couldn't be the owner.

Dennis gripped the item in this hand for a moment, wanting to wrap it around Stephanie's neck and squeeze tight. Instead he threw it against the wall. She'd been using him all these years, and he'd never suspected it. No wonder she didn't care about Jason Ward. She'd already found his replacement, and in case anything happened to Dennis, she'd already been on the market. She didn't care if he went down. But he wasn't going to. He wouldn't let anyone make a fool of him again. Not Jason, and certainly not some nobody like Abby Baylor. He'd go to that cocktail party and make sure she knew who she was dealing with.

Chapter 15

She'd lost. She'd lost the bet. Abby kicked off her shoes and fell onto her couch. The evening had started off with such promise. Jason had looked fabulous in his suit, and she'd felt amazing in her new dress. Little did she know that a night of drinking and networking would end in the local police station. Abby could just imagine Judith's smug face when pictures of the incident went public. No doubt someone would soon post a fuzzy video online of Jason that would go viral. She'd lose the office, and her reputation. It didn't matter that business at Southern Taste had tripled due to her efforts and help from a friend. Having her name linked with Jason Ward was definitely bad for business. It had been a sucker's bet.

The worst part was that he'd gotten into this mess to save her. Why couldn't he have just been a playboy? It would have been easier if he'd had some indiscretion—she could clean up after and put him in a new light. Or if he were a jackass, she could use that to his advantage. Even if he'd just been coarse and uncouth, she could polish that, and she had. But an urban warrior? He was a man from

another time—his sense of duty and honor was almost me-
dieval, a long-gone, forgotten art for most modern men.
A civilized man would have just thrown some words. A
brutal man would have just thrown some punches. Jason
had combined the two. All because of her.

Abby still wracked her brain, wondering what she could
have done differently. How could she have avoided what
happened? Everything had been going smoothly, starting
when he'd picked her up that evening. "You look amazing," he'd said, then frowned. "But…"

"But what?"

"Wait, you're missing something," he said, then presented her with a small jewelry box.

"But you've bought me enough things already."

"I know. But tonight you are going to be my queen, and
you'll need these."

Abby opened the box to find a pair of delicate diamond-
studded ruby earrings. She hadn't planned on wearing any
jewelry, but she had to admit he had taste. She pulled out
a small powder compact from her purse and had him hold
it up while she put on the earrings. They looked perfect.

Prior to the charity event, Abby had managed to get in
touch with the two businesses Jason had mentioned were
interested in his proposal. As soon as they entered the
ball, the lapel pin worked, becoming an easy conversation
starter. He opted to wear the one in the shape of a wishbone. He looked gorgeous and played the part of the newly
remade Jason Ward. He averted his gaze when necessary,
instead of using his typical laser-like stare, had improved
his handshake and she'd even seen a slight smile. People
seemed to feel less uneasy with him.

There had been tension when his ex-business partner,
Dennis Collins, had shown up. Whispers followed, but to
her relief, Jason stayed in control, remained calm, offered

him a cool greeting and left it at that. Fearing any problems, she'd even offered to leave.

"We've done enough socializing, so we don't have to stay longer," she'd said.

"I'm not leaving because of him."

"No one would blame you if you did."

"This isn't his usual thing. I'm curious to see what he is up to."

Jason's curiosity should have been the first sign of trouble, but Abby hadn't been perceptive enough to recognize that, or that Dennis was not a man to be underestimated. She should have never accepted his casual attempt to chat. She should have ignored him instead. If she had ignored him, she wouldn't have found herself cornered in a hallway, trapped by a man with dark eyes.

"What's the deal with you and Ward?" Dennis asked in a venomous tone that had been as smooth as butter only a few minutes before.

Abby boldly stared back, determined to be calm. "What does that have to do with you?"

"It's a warning." He grabbed her wrist. "And I'm only going to give you one."

Abby tried to pull her wrist free, but his grip only tightened. "Let me go."

"What do you know?"

"What are you talking about?" she said, exasperated. He was obviously drunk, but she'd seen no signs of it before.

"You're not going to even tell me how much? Is that the game you're playing?"

"I'm not playing any games," Abby said, looking around to see if she could get anyone's attention, but no one was around. "I don't know what you're talking about."

"Leave things alone."

"I said let go."

Dennis flashed an ugly grin and let his eyes trail the length of her. "I've got to give him credit. Jason always gets the lookers. Women like you who will do anything for him. One day I'll find out his secret."

"You could start by acting like a man instead of a boy. Now, let me go, or I'll scream."

His eyes blazed with fury. "I am a man. More than he ever was. I loved her, and he took her away from me. Do you know how she died?"

"Who?" Abby asked, a fissure of fear coursing through her as she looked at the tinge of madness in Dennis's gaze.

"Gwen. The only woman we'll ever love. But then, if he can get over her, maybe so can I," he said softly. As the look of madness grew, so did his sensual desire.

Abby couldn't understand his rapid change of emotion, but knew she didn't want to become his warped object of affection. "I don't care," she said, then stomped on his instep.

He swore, then slapped her—quick, like a flash.

"Apologize," Jason said, suddenly appearing out of no-where.

Dennis lowered his head. "You gonna make me?"

Jason sent Abby a quick, assessing glance, then said, "I'll write you a check," before he hauled Dennis to his feet as if he were a rag doll and shoved him against the wall. Before she knew what was happening, Jason was in handcuffs, Dennis was in an ambulance and she was being treated by EMTs and making a statement to the police, all the while wondering how she could salvage his reputation and hers.

Frantic, she called a close friend, a trauma nurse she knew at the hospital where Dennis had been taken, and told her what had happened. Her friend offered to help and provided Abby with information about how seriously Dennis had been injured. To her relief, other than his pride, Dennis would recover, with several bruised ribs and one cut that needed a couple of stitches. Jason could have done a lot more damage, but hadn't.

Abby promised her friend a free weekend at an exclusive spa retreat if she could get Dennis not to press charges. Then she called the two investors and let them know that the incident had been a misunderstanding and told them her story about being assaulted, and how Jason had come to her rescue. Thankfully, they both believed her and didn't challenge the authenticity of what she said. Next she contacted a local blogger she knew, and convinced him to put a spin on the event, putting Jason in a good light *without* tarnishing the other man's image. She didn't want Dennis to have any ammunition to sue Jason for defamation of character, especially since she didn't file assault charges against Dennis with the police.

"Quite an evening you had," Judith said when Abby showed up for work the next day.

She held up a hand, warding her off. "Don't start."

"You know your time is up."

"Yes, but I'm still not out."

"Why don't you just drop him and admit defeat?"

Thankfully Abby's phone rang, so she didn't have to reply. "Hello?"

"He won't press charges," her friend said.

"I won't even ask how you managed that."

"Let's just say that I'm going to use that spa retreat to wash myself clean. He's as slimy as they come, and dangerous."

"I know. Thanks."

Abby hung up the phone, then looked in her email and saw a message from one of the investors, wanting to follow up. The other individual hadn't replied yet, but that didn't bother her. If he was too squeamish, then he wouldn't be a good fit anyway. She sent a reply to the email and looked forward to telling Jason. She felt thrilled that she'd been able to divert a major disaster.

But then Jason disappeared.

Chapter 16

Three days. She hadn't been able to reach him for three lousy, long, horrible days. She couldn't reach him on his cell phone, and when she called his office, Benny wouldn't tell her anything. Where could he be? Why wouldn't he tell her where he was? She'd gotten the assault charge dropped, and this was how he repaid her? She'd been so close to winning the bet, and he'd ruined all her chances.

"You shouldn't have taken him on as a client in the first place," Judith said with a superior smile as she sat on the corner of Abby's desk and sipped iced tea. "I knew he'd be too much for you."

"I thought it was a good faith gesture," Abby said, pleased to hear her sister's true motive.

"It was," Judith quickly corrected. "But you were so eager to prove yourself. I told you he was a handful, but you just thought of the money, didn't you?"

"You won, okay? You always do, so why don't you go gloat somewhere else?"

"I'm glad I won, but I don't like to see you unhappy."

"It's sort of hard to believe someone when they have a smile on their face."

Judith tapped her mouth in a motion of remorse that she clearly didn't feel. "I'm sorry. It's just amazing that you thought you could change a man like that. At least it's over."

"It's not over."

Judith set her cup down. "What do you mean? The six weeks are up. You failed. Forget about him."

"No. He's still my client, and we still have a lot of work to do."

"Don't let pride get in the way. You don't have to prove anything to me. Listen, why don't we work together—"

"No, I'm not finished with Jason Ward."

But as the days passed, Jason's absence made it clear he was finished with her. Judith beamed with victory every time she saw Abby. And soon Abby started to wonder about her own motivation. Judith was right; she should move on. He'd forgotten about her, so she should forget about him. At first she'd wondered if he'd gone off the radar because he was embarrassed, but Jason didn't get embarrassed. Every reason she tried to come up with didn't work. The only explanation that made sense was that he didn't want to see her again, and that stung.

But she'd invested too much time and energy to stop now. She didn't care that she'd lost to her sister, but Judith's smug grin haunted her in her dreams. Jason meant more than a bet to her. She cared about him. She wanted to know if he was okay. She wanted to see his plan for the specialized resorts succeed.

Damn it, she just wanted to see him again and tell him what a bastard he was for treating her like this. She wanted to be the one to end things. That anger gave her the fuel she needed to continue her search and led her to the one man she knew owed her.

"Where is Jason?" she asked Henry after a quick meal of fried chicken masala. Southern Taste had become one of her favorite places to go.

He shrugged. "I don't know."

Abby folded her arms. "Guess."

"Abby, when things happen, like that big fight at that fancy event, he likes to be left alone."

"So you *do* know where he is?" she pressed.

Henry hesitated.

"Do you want me to tell your wife what happened in the alley?"

Henry briefly hung his head. "I knew that would come back to bite me." He sighed, then with reluctance said, "Okay, he took his mother out of town for a few days, but he should be back. And I know where he might be."

Jason assembled the bookshelf and rested it against the wall. Taking a break helping his mother arrange things in her house was a nice respite. She lived within walking distance to one of his vacation homes hidden away in the mountains in western Maryland. He had a caretaker who looked after the property when he was away. "Is this where you want it?"

"At least talk to her."

His mother had been asking him to contact Abby for the past several days. He still couldn't get that night out of his mind. She had opened her door, and had left him breathless. He'd given her a simple pair of earrings when he'd wanted to drown her in diamonds and pearls. She'd looked stunning in the red dress—a dress he imagined himself stripping her out of. But those pleasant memories were always hijacked by seeing Dennis assaulting her. He saw red. He wasn't surprised when the handcuffs were slapped on him; he just wished he could have checked to make sure Abby was fine before he was taken away.

Then the miraculous happened. He was let go. A police officer told him no charges had been filed. He knew that Abby must have been behind that. Dennis had never been charitable. Hell, he'd allowed him to go to federal prison. It got his mind working, and he wanted to see how far she would go. He was taking a risk by being out of reach, but knowing Abby, he figured it would be a challenge she'd take.

"I think I should move it over to that wall," he said.

"Jason," his mother warned.

"I will call her."

"When?"

"When the time is right."

"She's not one you should let get away."

"You've never met her. How do you know?" He shook his head and sighed as the answer came to him. "You've been talking to Rosemary."

"You took her there. That meant you were making a statement. You're serious about her."

"Yes."

"And does she feel the same?"

He hoped so. He hoped that all that had happened hadn't ruined things for him. He wanted her to see him in another light. Not just as a client, but as a man. *Her man.*

Abby checked the address again, hoping that Henry had given her the right one. The house didn't look as if it would suit Jason. It wasn't like his mansion. This one was too small and too simple, dusted with a light snow and decorated with lights for the holidays. She expected a man like Jason to have a much bigger, grander place to escape to. Instead, she found herself looking at a small ranch-style house that sat isolated and surrounded by several acres of land. She'd practiced what she'd say to him, but the words didn't seem adequate now. She had already done a lot, including getting the charges dropped, and several online blogs' help to bury the fiasco at the Madison Ball, but she still needed to get his image to a certain level so that he wouldn't always be so vulnerable.

Abby knocked on the door, and a dowdy woman with dark eyes opened it. "Can I help you?"

"I'm here to see Jason," she said in a formal tone.

"And you are?"

"Here to see him," Abby said, unused to the staff getting personal.

The woman narrowed her eyes. "Try again. You won't get past me with an attitude like that."

She had attitude to spare, but Abby knew the woman was right. "I'm Abby, and I'm here to speak to Mr. Ward about business." That was all she'd tell her. She didn't know if Jason wanted anyone to know she'd been hired by him or why.

"He's not here."

Abby sighed. Maybe it was time for her to give up. She'd cleaned up a nasty scandal, and now he'd disappeared. Maybe it was good if he stayed gone. "Okay."

"But he'll be back in about ten minutes if you can wait that long."

"I'll wait."

The woman reluctantly opened the door wider. "Come in."

"Thank you." Abby followed the woman into a small sitting room and took a seat. The woman sat, too, without offering any refreshments, and Abby didn't want to ask. She was a surly woman, and Abby didn't want to upset her. She appeared to be well matched for Jason. Maybe she wasn't used to having visitors and didn't know how to behave, Abby thought, feeling a little uncomfortable but determined not to show it. She was in desperate need of manners, but Abby wasn't going to teach her. One unruly client was enough.

"You don't have to lie to me," the woman said.

"Lie?"

"Yes, are you really here to see Jason for business?"

"Yes."

The woman raised her brows. "You sure it's not something more?"

You sure it's any of your business? "Yes, he hired me."

"What do you do?"

"I work with branding companies." That was vague enough. Abby did not feel the need to expand.

"Ms., I—" Benny said, coming into the room. He stopped when he saw Abby. "Does he know she's here?"

"He will soon," the woman said. "I assume you know each other?"

"Yes," Abby said.

"Yes," Benny said, then quickly added, "She's been helping Jason with a lot of stuff."

"With his business image," Abby said, not wanting her work referred to as "stuff."

"Hmm…he could certainly use that. The moment he opens his mouth, he gets on someone's bad side."

Abby just smiled. She wasn't going to bad-mouth him. If she wanted his reputation to be stellar, she had to guard it. "He's improving."

"Slowly. He's got a nasty temper and a filthy mouth. Isn't that right, Benny?"

"Yes."

"He's also incredibly bright and kind," Abby countered.

"Kind? Ever see him make a grown man cry?" The woman giggled. "He is awful."

"Only when he needs to be. I don't deny that he can appear to be a little rough around the edges—" Abby did not like someone working for Jason to be talking badly about him.

"He's all edges. As cutting as a double-edged sword."

"Yeah," Benny added. "He'll slice you to the quick."

"But he's got integrity, which is rare these days," Abby said.

The woman narrowed her eyes. "What did you say your name was again?"

"Abby Baylor." She held out her hand. "I apologize, I should have introduced myself sooner. It's just that I have a lot on my mind."

The woman looked at her outstretched hand and kept her arms folded. "You don't have to pretend with me. I know he can be a mean SOB."

"I'll just finish up out back," Benny said, sensing the tension in the room. When no one replied, he turned and left.

Abby let her neglected hand fall and sighed. "I'm not pretending. But I prefer to focus on his better qualities."

The woman looked at Abby with renewed interest. "That's rare, too. Most people like tearing successful men down, especially men like Jason. And with a lower-class background like his. You know about his background, right?"

Abby stiffened. Why did people keep bringing up his background? Henry had also mentioned it briefly. People couldn't help where they came from. "His background is none of my business."

"You're not even curious?"

She was very curious. Curious about the woman he'd once loved. She was curious about what he liked to eat for breakfast and what it was like to wake up to him. But she had no intention of sharing her curiosity with anyone, least of all this nondescript woman sitting in front of her. Besides, the fact that he'd dropped her obviously showed he had little interest in her. "What he does in the present is all that matters to me."

"I didn't want to like you, but I do. I don't care what others say about a person. I like to find out for myself." She held out her hand. "I'm Beatrice. Would you like anything to drink?"

"I'm fine," Abby said, shaking her hand and stumbling over her words. "Thank you."

All of a sudden, a full smile swept over the woman's face, making it look warm and less dowdy, a welcoming change to the coldness she had been greeted with.

Suddenly Abby noticed a beautiful knitted scarf lying on the center table. She leaned down and picked it up. "This is gorgeous."

"I like to knit in my spare time. I didn't think it was for me. You know, knitting is something old biddies do to keep busy, but it keeps me calm. I only started six months ago."

"But you're very good. You know, we could use some small knitted items for the premature babies in our neonatal unit at the hospital." Abby immediately explained to Beatrice about her volunteering at the hospital and the need for customized items to fit them. "Would you be interested?"

"Yes, I'd love to."

"Should I come back?" Jason asked. The two women jumped when he spoke. They had been so busy talking, they hadn't noticed him come in.

Beatrice smiled at him. "I was keeping Abby company. I'll go see what we can have for dinner." She got up quickly and left.

Abby toyed with the hem of her shirt, suddenly not knowing what to do. She'd come prepared to be angry with him, but the casually dressed man in blue jeans and gray shirt reminded her of the man in the restaurant who'd made her mouth drool. It annoyed her to be so happy again, but she was. However, she had to focus. "Your housekeeper is great," she said, knowing that compliments always helped a conversation. "I really like her. I wasn't sure I would. When I first met her, I found her to be fierce, but I'm sure she picked up bad habits from you."

Jason scratched the side of his cheek, amused. "Actually, it's the other way around."

"You picked up habits from her?"

Jason sat down beside her. "Yes, she's my mother."

Abby opened her mouth then closed it, her face burning.

Jason laughed. "It's okay. She likes to make people think that. This is where I come to get away. She has a small house a few yards away. I wanted to get her a bigger place, but she likes living there."

"A bigger house would be harder to clean," Beatrice said, coming back into the living room, carrying a tray filled with refreshments.

"You wouldn't have to do any cleaning. I'd get you a maid."

"I'm fine. I like a house I can manage." She grabbed her purse. "I'm going shopping for dinner because there's not enough here."

"Mom, we can take care of ourselves."

Her gaze darted between them, then she sent her son a significant look as if to say "behave," before she said goodbye.

Once his mother had gone, Jason leaned back on the couch and grinned at Abby. "I wondered how long it would take for you to find me."

"Why did you just disappear?"

He stretched his arm the length of the couch, then let his fingers toy with the back of her collar. "I had to take Mom away for a while and think about a few things."

She pushed his hand away, although his fingers made her skin tingle. "You could have told me."

"I couldn't. So, how did you do it?"

"Do what?"

"Get that weasel Dennis to drop the charges?"

"I have a friend who works at the hospital who can be very persuasive. And I got an email from investor number one. He still wants in on the business venture. I'm not sure if TriStar Medicals will still consider working with you. We'll have to wait and see."

He twirled a strand of her hair at the nape of her neck around his finger. "Great."

Abby moved his hand away, determined to stay on topic, although her heart continued to pick up its pace. "I just know how to charm people, and you will, too, if you'll give me another chance. You'll be able to do exactly what I just did."

He shook his head. "I don't have the time to learn. I'm a busy man."

"I know that, and I already know a strategy that will work."

"If I continue working with you, I want to be your only client for the next several weeks."

Abby paused. That was a gamble, but she didn't have many clients anyway, and she wanted to work with him as long as she could. "That's fine."

"And I want you to be my good manners."

"What?"

"I saw you at work at the Madison Ball, and I just don't have the patience for that. I have a lot I want to accomplish, and I know that you can help me. The networking you did was amazing. People may be afraid of me, but they trust you, and they'll talk to you to get to me."

"But I'm a coach."

"I'll learn by example." Jason quickly wrote something down, then handed it to her.

Abby looked at the figure, and her eyes widened. "Per month?"

"Per week. You believe in what I'm doing, and I want to make things happen. I don't want my past or my personality to stand in the way. Agreed?"

"Yes."

"I'll send you a contract tomorrow."

"Okay."

"On one condition."

"What?"

His eyes held hers, and his voice deepened with a velvet thread of warning. "You tell me the real reason why you came here."

Abby licked her lips, her insides trembling. "I told you."

"Because I'm your client?"

"Yes."

"Business that bad?"

"I was worried about you."

"So, you want to pretend the other night never happened?"

"I think it's best, don't you?" she said in a rush. "If we're going to work together, it will be better for both of us. You keep breaking the rules. You swore. You stared him down, and I told you not to fight."

Jason frowned, confused. "What did you expect me to do?"

"I could have handled him."

Jason lightly brushed the back of her neck. "He wasn't getting the hint fast enough."

Abby pushed his hand away, resisting the urge to lean back farther. "This is why people think you're an out-of-control hothead."

"What did you expect me to do? Just watch him take advantage of you?"

"You could have talked to him."

His voice cracked in surprise. "Are you serious?"

"I'm sure there was another solution," Abby said, knowing her words sounded lame.

"Like what?"

She threw up her hands, irritated that he could make her feel both aroused and furious at the same time. Why couldn't he see how important the Madison Ball had been for his image? "I don't know. But I still can't believe you got into a fight. Especially at such a public event."

"He slapped you," he said in a flat tone.

"Because he was drunk."

Jason shook his head. "He wasn't drunk."

"He had to be. He was saying the craziest things about me leaving him alone, and Gwen."

Jason paused. "He talked about Gwen?"

"Yes, how you both loved her."

Jason's jaw twitched. "He shouldn't have mentioned that."

"He found out when you kicked him in the back of the knees and forced him to the ground. I've never seen a move like that before."

He looked at her in surprise. "Never?"

"In a movie maybe, but not in real life. I mean, you acted like…" *Like a hero,* she silently finished.

"Like what?"

"Never mind. It was my fault. I shouldn't have walked out with him to such an isolated place. But I was just curious."

Jason's eyes flashed fire, but his tone remained cold. "He shouldn't have touched you."

Abby bit her lip. "I shouldn't have done what I did and hurt him."

Jason's eyes widened. "You grabbed his pinkie?"

Abby laughed. "No, but I should have. I crushed his instep. That's when he slapped me, but I'm okay now," she quickly added when she saw Jason's jaw tighten. "I'm glad it's over."

Jason lightly cupped her face. "Is it still sore?" he said with such tenderness her heart melted.

"I've never mixed business with pleasure," she said. "But I'd like to finish what we started in your house." Then she kissed him, surrendering to the raging hunger she felt. She removed his clothes with a ferocity that surprised them both, but Jason didn't stop her. She licked him, kissed him, tasted him all over. She'd never wanted a man this much. Every touch of his was gentle, but to her it was sweet agony. She wanted him rough and raw, and she showed him the way and soon found herself reveling in the warmth of his soft flesh.

He picked her up and took her to the bedroom, where Jason removed her shirt with the same ferocity she'd used to remove his, then laid her on the bed and covered her with his body. He was large, like a tidal wave, and she welcomed him inside her, an aching need now satiated by his hot arousal. Although he was big, no part of him frightened her. His hands roamed over her, making her gasp in pleasure, his warm, wet mouth causing her senses to whirl.

Moments later they lay weak and exhausted in each other's arms, their legs intertwined. Jason stared up at the ceiling, knowing that if he looked at the woman lying next to him, he'd want to make love to her all over again. But there wasn't enough time. His mother would be returning soon.

She fit him. He never thought he'd meet another woman who would. She matched his passion; his desire would never overwhelm her. It was an intoxicating feeling. She didn't need him to change and accepted him as he was. He was glad her ex was stupid enough to let her go. He'd make sure to keep her safe, permanently.

Abby lightly touched his face. "I want to protect you."

Jason laughed, wondering if she'd somehow read his thoughts. "Protect me? I'm going to protect you."

She shook her head. "No one knows how wonderful you really are."

He shrugged and grinned. "With you by my side, I don't care anymore."

She bit her lip.

"What?"

"When you're ready, you know you can tell me anything."

"Such as?"

"Your past. Your time in prison. I know it's a painful subject," she said quickly. "But I just want you to know that I'm here for you. I know what it's like to not be believed."

He turned to her sharply, hearing the pain in her voice. "What happened? Did someone hurt you?"

Abby sighed. "It's nothing as bad as what happened to you."

"Tell me anyway."

"Charles told everyone he had done everything on his own. Seven years of my life down the drain because everyone believed he had built his company up all on his own. I was just the pretty wife who hosted parties and lived well. Nobody knew I was instrumental in making sure all his meetings with key investors and executives went well. I was the one with the big vision for the business. I helped make it grow. But everyone believed his lies because I don't have the right degrees. It wasn't just the prenuptial that hurt me. If he'd admitted, just once, that he used me, or even if he'd said, 'Thank you, you did a good job' one time, that would have meant something."

Jason's hand slid down her leg. "When we're in bed, I don't want you to think of anyone else but me."

Abby laughed, then kissed him.

"What was that for?"

Abby hugged him, resting her head on his chest and sighing with pleasure. "This is a great consolation prize."

"Consolation prize?"

She lifted her head and made a face. "I shouldn't have said anything."

"It's too late now."

"You know you've cost me a lot of money. I made a bet with my sister, and I lost."

"What was the bet?"

"That I could transform you into a civilized gentleman in six weeks. I was certain I could, but she didn't think so, and she was right."

He rested an arm behind his head. "You should have listened to her."

"She lets me know that every day," Abby said with a groan.

"How much did you lose?"

"I have to pay the rent for my office for the next six months, and I could hardly afford my half. Fortunately, my new position with you will make it possible. Unless…"

"Unless what?"

"If you hadn't disappeared, I may have won, so you owe me."

His eyes twinkled with amusement. "Admit that you lost. You can't completely civilize me."

She sighed. "You're right."

"I'll pay, since I'm the reason you lost your bet, but don't let your sister know."

"I won't. Trust me. I wish I didn't have to see her every day. At least for a while."

"You won't have to. We have a lot of work to do. Is your passport up to date?"

"Yes."

"Good, because we're going to the islands."

Chapter 17

"Yes, she found him and she's even better than you said," Beatrice said to Rosemary over the phone.

"I told you."

"I wasn't sure. I tried my best to get her to say nasty things about him, and she wouldn't."

"I know."

"Even when Benny agreed with me, she wouldn't mention a thing."

"That's a rare trait."

"She told me that he's smart and a man of integrity. I've finally met a woman who sees my son the way we do."

"She's nothing like Gwen."

"I know. That's what surprised me the most. Gwen had been like sunshine—warm and bright. Abby isn't like that."

"But she isn't exactly cold," Rosemary said in defense. "I instantly liked her."

"I'm sure that was only because she liked your cooking. But for the rest of us, she takes a little getting used to. She thought I was his maid."

Rosemary laughed. "I bet you made her think that, too."

"I wanted to see how she'd respond. People act different when they think they're talking to the help. At first I thought she was being condescending because she thought I was a maid, until I realized she was protecting Jason."

"Has she met Blues Man yet?"

"I'm sure he's keeping them apart until the right moment."

"How do you think she'll react?"

"I'm not sure. She's not predictable."

"You've got that right. Do you think she realizes she loves him yet?"

"No, but knowing my son, she'll find out soon."

The life of luxury she'd dreamed about had finally come true again. Their trip to Cape Verde started with them flying on a private jet to one of the little islands where Jason had reserved a villa. The heavenly beaches surrounding the island provided a number of opportunities to participate in a variety of water sports, including wind and kite-surfing, and diving. Abby had never gone windsurfing before, and was excited when Jason said he'd make sure to sign her up for lessons.

The next day, they woke up early and went on a fishing expedition. The chef at the villa cooked what they caught that day for their evening meal. But what they liked the most was that there were no large crowds of tourists to deal with. They were able to have a lot of time to themselves and enjoy their surroundings. The villa they stayed in provided an oceanfront view that afforded them the luxury of waking up to see the sunrise and watch the sunset in the evenings.

The food was like none she had ever experienced before. Every day they were treated to excellent fish and seafood dishes, including grilled lobster soaked in olive oil. And they tried octopus and stingray, and other fish eaten as a delicacy by the locals. They sampled a delicious stew called Cachupa, which was made using tuna or marinated pork, corn, beans, carrots, tomatoes and spices. Jason tried and got used to drinking one of the favorite drinks of the locals called Grogue, made from cane sugar, coffee, lime and cinnamon.

One of the main features they enjoyed was the coastline that appeared to go on forever. The island wasn't as developed as other more visited areas in Cape Verde, and that suited them just right. They could walk along the beach and spend time in each other's arms, or walk along one of the beaches where the dunes ran down to the water, and lie in the soft white sand. The sparkling, crystalline waters glistened in different tones of blue and turquoise. In one of the local craft shops, Jason bought her a marble statue of a fisherman she'd been eyeing.

On day four of their vacation, Jason signed them up for windsurfing lessons; Abby didn't want to try kitesurfing or scuba diving. She decided to wear a bright yellow linen shorts set that looked great against her brown skin. They spent several days enjoying the sport, and in the evening, paid close attention to each other, carefully applying first aid ointment to some of the bruises they got along the way. On the final day of their trip, Jason rented a four-by-four and drove Abby to Santa Mónica beach. It was difficult to access but worth the effort, with a long stretch of sand. All day they went swimming, lazed out in the sun under the tent he had brought and ate a sumptuous lunch he'd had specially packed by their chef.

"When did you first know?" Abby teased once they had finished eating. The fresh scent of the sea air mingled with the soft sounds of the water.

"When did I first know what?"

"That you couldn't resist me?"

Jason stared out at the water, and a quick grin touched the corner of his mouth.

When he didn't speak, she nudged him. "Come on, tell me."

"The moment I met you."

"I remember when I first saw you, I thought you were beautiful. Then you opened your mouth and ruined everything."

"In the office?"

Abby shook her head. "No, it was before that. I saw you in a restaurant."

"What was I saying?"

Abby cringed. "I can't repeat it, but let's just say you were on the phone, and you were very angry."

He laughed. "I have gotten better."

"Because there's been no one to swear at. When are you going to tell me more about Gwen?"

Jason sighed, and the light in his eyes dimmed. "There's not much to tell. I loved her and she died."

"That's it?"

His gaze shifted to the rolling waves and the blue sky. "What more do you want to know?"

"What she was like. How did you meet?" *How did she die?*

"Why?"

"Because then I'll know more about you."

He turned to her and captured her eyes with his, their dark intensity holding her still. "I'm not hiding anything. You know everything you need to."

Except how it feels to be loved by you, Abby wanted to say. She knew he enjoyed her. He liked her, especially in bed. But at times, he still seemed out of reach. What had made him love Gwen? How different were they? Why did she care? But she already knew the answer. Because she loved him. After Charles and another relationship that had been short-lived, she'd never thought she'd lose her heart again, but now she had, to a man who could thrill and infuriate her at the same time.

"Okay," she said, not wanting to ruin the beautiful day by bringing up a subject that pained them both. "I won't ask any more questions."

"The future is all that matters to me now, not the past."

What future? she wanted to ask, but didn't. Was this just an affair or something more? How long would their partnership continue? Did it really matter? She felt a little foolish that she'd given her heart to him so freely when he'd offered her no promises. But she couldn't alter her feelings, so she'd have to alter his by not putting too much pressure on him. She needed him to see how much he needed her, and she would start now. Being useful had always worked before.

"So, when do we start working?" she asked.

"We already have been. The villa we are staying in belongs to me. Also the craft store we stopped in, and I now own several of the water sporting companies, who have all agreed to make sure they can accommodate a wide range of guests and their special needs."

"Oh."

"What do you think?"

"I think that's wonderful. I had no idea people with special needs would be able to come to a place like this and enjoy themselves, without having to worry about their health needs. I'd love to see more of the island."

He stood. "Then let's go."

That last day of their holiday, they decided to drive along the cliffs and valleys of the island, enjoying the landscape and taking photographs. That evening, as they turned toward the main road to their villa, they saw a car in front of them cross the divide and plunge into the water. Jason quickly pulled to the side. After several heart-stopping seconds, he saw a young woman come up out of the water screaming, "My baby! My baby! She's still in the car!"

Chapter 18

Abby jumped out of the car, kicked off her shoes, ran toward the woman and dove into the water. Twice she went under and couldn't see the car, then the third time she did. Fortunately, the water wasn't too deep, and she was able to see where it had landed and swim toward it. She slipped through the opened door where the mother had been able to escape and spotted the baby in the car seat—motionless. She didn't let that bother her. She only had so much time before she needed air. She had to remain calm. She'd been able to hold her breath at the pool and knew she'd strengthened her lungs enough to do this task.

She undid the latch of the car seat and pulled the baby out. She looked to the light dancing on the surface of the water and swam toward it, feeling her resolve shaking. She needed air and broke through the water just when she thought she wouldn't make it. She could feel her lungs burn, and her arms ached, but none of that mattered. She had to get the baby to shore and give it CPR.

She carried the limp form to land and handed the baby over to Jason before she collapsed from exhaustion. Jason grabbed the lifeless body and felt for a pulse. There was none. "Call for help," he told the mother, cutting her panicky cries and screams with a swift command.

"You need to calm down, if we're going to save your baby," Abby said in a softer tone. She pulled out her cell phone from her purse and handed it to the woman. "Here. Just dial zero. I'm not sure what the code is for the island."

"But she's not breathing!"

Abby waved the phone at her. "Do it. Just dial."

The woman whimpered and dialed, giving the emergency response team instructions on where to find them.

Jason positioned the child's small body down on the sand, and began to perform CPR. It seemed like forever before they heard the sound of sirens, but it had only been about four minutes.

"We'll take over, sir," one of the EMTs said as they continued CPR. They put the child on a stretcher, then helped the mother into the ambulance. Jason and Abby watched, exhausted and terrified, as the ambulance drove away, hoping and wishing that the child would survive.

When cameras and reporters arrived on their doorstep that night, they learned that the child would be okay. Thanks to Abby's swift reaction and Jason starting CPR, the child was expected to make a full recovery and had suffered no damage as a result of the accident.

The story of the rescue quickly spread, not only on the island, but online. After giving brief statements to the hungry reporters, they packed up their things and flew out early the next morning.

A hero? They were calling him a hero? Dennis stared at the computer screen in stunned amazement. One of the stories was titled *Tourists Save Local Child*. He'd watched the shaky camera phone image of the rescue, and there was no denying who the people were: Jason Ward and Abby Baylor. Their daring action and swift thinking made them heroes, and the story was sweeping the news. But even though Dennis knew what they did would count for just a second of fame, he couldn't stand it. Jason Ward wasn't a hero. He was an ex-con. A man removed from his own company because he intimidated everyone. Dennis looked at the last image of Jason and Abby hugging each other and smiling. Why were they smiling? Were they smiling because of the rescue, or because they knew something?

Would Abby keep her mouth shut? He was still consumed with worry. What exactly did she know? Judith had said Abby had damaging information. It could be anything. Were they planning something? That sweet nurse at the hospital had convinced him not to press charges, but now he wondered if he should have. At times he thought he heard people whispering behind his back and looking at him before turning away. Did anyone else suspect something? And he'd heard rumors that Jason's company had partnered with a major medical supply company. How had he managed that? He couldn't have done that alone.

Abby had something to do with it. He was sure of it. Were they both laughing at him? He had to make sure that Abby knew he meant business. Maybe she hadn't gotten the message when he'd met with her at the party. He picked up the phone, then dialed a number he hadn't called in years.

"Hello?" a dark, sinister voice asked.

"I have a job for you."

"Hello, stranger," Judith said, coming into Abby's office. A light, cold January rain tapped against the window.

"I'm hardly a stranger," Abby said. She sat behind her desk, going through her mail. She didn't bother to look up.

Judith sat on the corner of Abby's desk. "It's been several weeks since your vacation, but you're hardly in the office these days."

Her sister was right. Since Christmas dinner with the family, she'd spent most of her time with Jason on chauffeur-driven excursions, eating in fine restaurants, travelling, going on shopping sprees and other delights. "Doesn't that make you happy?"

"I thought your business was important. It's not like you to have one man monopolize your time."

"No one is monopolizing my time."

Judith shrugged, unconvinced, and stood, knocking over the statue Abby had sitting there. The one Jason had bought her on the island. It tumbled to the ground, and the figure snapped off.

Judith picked it up. "Oh, I'm sorry."

Abby snatched the two broken pieces from her. "Why can't you be more careful?"

"Why did you have it on your desk? If it was so important, you should have placed it somewhere else."

Abby dropped the pieces in a drawer and slammed it shut.

"I could get you some glue."

Abby waved her stack of mail at Judith, although most of it was junk. "Can't you see I'm busy?"

"You haven't been the same since…" She let her words trail off.

"Since what?"

"Jason Ward."

Abby clasped her hands together and kept her voice low. "If you have something to say, just say it."

Judith sat down and shook her head. "You're so happy with him, it's almost sad."

"Why sad?"

"Haven't you done all this before? Didn't your divorce teach you anything?"

"What does my divorce have to do with anything?"

"I guess love is making you blind."

"Stop trying to sound clever and tell me what you want to say."

"I just don't want to see you hurt."

Abby rested her chin in her hand. "I'm listening."

"He's using you, just like Charles did."

"He's not using me. This is business."

"Really? Does a client usually buy you new clothes and take you out to fancy restaurants and shows? And on an island vacation?"

"We also happen to be in a relationship."

"Exactly. Once his business is where he wants it, he'll drop you just like Charles did. You think you're indispensable, but you're not," she said, then left.

Abby stuck her tongue out at her sister, then opened her drawer and removed the broken pieces. She could glue it, maybe. But the sculpture would never be the same. Just like her sister's words would never make her see her relationship with Jason in the same light. In seconds, the objects in her hands were blurred by tears. She jumped when someone knocked on the door. She quickly blinked and stared up at the figure in the door. She smiled when she realized it was Jason.

He didn't smile back. "What happened?"

Abby thought about plastering on a smile, then thought better of it. She held up the broken statue. "It fell."

He walked to the desk and held out his hands. She handed the pieces to him. "I think I can glue it."

"How did it break?"

"My sister accidentally knocked it over."

"Are you sure it was an accident?"

"Don't be mean."

He lifted a sly brow. "Remember, I've met your sister." He leaned down over her desk and kissed her, then leaned back. "I'll get you another one."

"Thanks."

"What else made you unhappy?"

Abby narrowed her eyes. "Are you trying to become a mind reader?"

"No, it's just that a broken statue isn't enough to make you cry."

Abby waved the thought aside. "Oh, it's nothing." She sighed. "I just had a sisterly chat with Judith. She said—"

Jason swore. "Stop. I don't want to know."

Abby stared at him for a moment. "But you just said—"

"I changed my mind. Don't tell me."

She laughed, amused by the fierceness of his words. "You're not even curious?"

"Your sister broke your statue and made you cry. Do you want me to be even angrier at her?"

"The statue was an accident."

"Do you want me to hate her?"

"No."

"Then don't tell me what she said." He lifted Abby to her feet and wrapped his arms around her waist, holding her close. "Let me put you in a better mood," he said, his gaze as soft as a caress before his mouth covered hers.

"Abby," Judith called from the main office entrance. "I'm sorry about the statue, but I'm not sorry about Jason being all wrong—" Her words died away when she saw them together. She took a hasty step back. "I didn't know you'd come in," she stammered.

"Why don't you finish what you were going to say?" Jason said in an ominous tone.

"It's nothing," she said in a high, nervous voice, taking

another step back. "I'll leave you two alone." She hurried out of the room.

Jason pulled Abby close. "What did she say that made you cry?"

"Nothing."

"But she made you question me."

Abby pressed her hands against his chest, trying to push him back. He didn't move. "Please, Jason, it's nothing. She was just teasing me, but I didn't get the joke." Abby shook her head, embarrassed that he'd caught her at a vulnerable time. "She's just worried about me. That's what sisters do."

He swore, then sighed. "Fine. Let me take you to lunch."

She toyed with the buttons of his shirt. "Can't you finish putting me in a better mood?" she asked, closing the door to her office and locking it, making sure her hips made her message clear.

"Yes, I can do that," Jason said, and in minutes they forgot about Judith, and lunch.

Chapter 19

Judith was a problem he would handle, Jason thought as he checked his place one more time to make sure it was ready for Abby's visit. But not tonight. Tonight he wanted to spend another evening with Abby and celebrate another successful deal. He wondered when she would discover that she was no longer just acting as his good manners, but that she had the charm and savvy of a formidable businesswoman. He'd convince her of that later, but tonight he didn't want to think about anything but a good meal and a fun night in bed. He'd sent Benny away, the table was set and dinner would arrive in thirty minutes.

Someone rang the doorbell. Jason quickly checked his reflection in the mirror before he answered with a smile.

But Abby wasn't standing on the other side of the door. Blues Man was. He took one look at Jason and started to laugh. "Man, what you doing wearing green?" He walked past him and slapped him on the back. "What are you? A leprechaun!"

Jason frowned and closed the door. "Wrong month. Abby got me this shirt."

"And it looks good on you. You know I'm playing. I'm just not used to you wearing color."

"What do you want?"

"I thought we could hang out." He glanced around the place Jason used when he was in the city, then his gaze fell on the table decorated with flowers and candles. "But it looks like you're expecting company. Abby?"

"Glad you got the hint." Jason opened the front door, then heard heels coming down the hallway. He quickly peeked his head out and saw Abby. He swore. He wouldn't be able to get rid of his cousin before she came. He closed the door and pointed at him. "Behave yourself."

Blues Man held up his hands. "Don't you trust me?"

"No. I'm going to introduce you, and then you're going to leave."

His cousin smiled. Jason knew that wasn't a good sign, but he didn't have enough time to argue. He sent his cousin one last warning look, then answered the door when Abby knocked.

"Is something wrong?" she asked after he kissed her. "I saw you peek your head out, then you closed the door."

"I just wanted to make sure the place was perfect."

She wrapped her arms around his neck and winked. "If you're in the room, I'm not thinking about the furniture."

Jason slid his arms around her waist, ready to deepen the kiss he'd first given her, when Blues Man loudly cleared his throat behind him. Jason briefly shut his eyes and swore. He let Abby go and turned to his cousin.

"A friend of mine just dropped by, and he's leaving now."

Blues Man came forward and shook Abby's hand. "My cousin's being modest. We're friends, but also family. You must be Abby. Jason has told me a lot about you. Don't worry, I know you can't say the same."

Abby smiled. "It's a pleasure to meet you...?"

He took her hand, tucked it through his arm and led her to the living room. "Just call me Blues Man. Jason, why don't you get those drinks while I keep Abby company?"

Jason shot him a glance that his cousin ignored. Jason swore again but didn't do as his cousin asked. Instead he followed the pair and sat in between them, forcing his cousin to take the seat across from Abby. His cousin lifted his brow in a sign of respect, knowing that Jason had staked his claim, but sat back as if he didn't intend to leave, at least not yet.

"Well, I have to say you've done a lot for my cousin," Blues Man said. "I didn't think I'd live to see him wearing colors again."

"Oh, that part was easy," Abby said. "Getting him to wear a suit was another story."

"You got my cuz to wear a three-piece? Do you have pictures?"

"Yes, wait a minute. I think I have a couple on my phone." She showed him the pictures that had gone viral following the fight.

He laughed.

"So, what kind of name is Blues Man?" Abby asked.

Blues Man rested his arm on the back of the chair. "The only one I respond to."

"It's a very unique name. Are you into jazz?"

He grinned. "I give people the blues, but I'm not into jazz."

"So what do you do?"

"I'm a businessman."

"Oh, it must run in the family."

Jason rested his arm behind Abby's head and checked his watch. "Yes, and speaking of running, don't you have to be somewhere?"

"It can wait," Blues Man said. "It's not every day that I get to meet an intelligent, beautiful woman."

Abby blushed. "It's not every day I get a compliment like that."

"Then my cuz must be slipping, because I'd let you know that every day," he said in a velvety tone.

Jason's gaze darkened, and he gave his cousin a foul gesture over Abby's shoulder. When he pointed at him, Blues Man got the message.

"Yes, but we're talking about business, right?" he said, wisely changing his approach. "Cuz and I like to work for ourselves. We like that freedom."

"What kind of business do you do?" Abby asked.

"I own several."

Abby leaned forward, excited. "I've always been fascinated by serial entrepreneurs. I'd love to talk about—"

"He doesn't have the time," Jason cut in.

"Yes, I'm a busy man," Blues Man added.

"But what's your main area of interest?" Abby asked.

"Finance. I handle loans."

"Really? Maybe we could work together and—"

"No," Jason said with such force that she jumped.

She turned to him, startled. "Why not?"

He glared at his cousin. "Get out now."

"Jason, don't be rude."

Blues Man slowly rose to his feet. "It's okay. It's a family thing. I don't blame Jason for wanting to keep you all to himself."

"It was wonderful to meet you," Abby said, also standing and shaking his hand.

He pulled her forward and gave her a quick peck on the cheek. "We'll meet again."

Jason shoved him toward the door. "I'll get you for this," he said under his breath.

His cousin laughed. "She's worth it."

Jason opened the door, and saw a young man holding a delivery box.

"Hey, dinner smells good," Blues Man said.

"Why don't you stay for dinner?" Abby said behind them.

Jason gave the deliveryman a tip, then said in a low voice, "If you say yes, I'll make sure you choke on your first bite."

Blues Man turned to Abby with a smile of regret. "I wish I could, but I really gotta run." He stepped out the door and turned to Jason, but before he could say any more, Jason closed the door in his face.

Abby stared at him, stunned. "Why did you do that?"

"Because I'm ready to eat," Jason said, taking Abby by the elbow and walking to the set table.

"He looked like he wanted to tell you something."

He pulled out her chair. "He can tell me later."

"I liked him."

"Hmm." He placed the food on the table, then sat. "Let's talk about something else."

Abby took the hint and changed the subject. After they enjoyed their dinner of chicken cacciatore, they watched a movie, then made love. Jason felt himself drifting off to sleep with Abby's legs still curled around him, her head on his chest, when she said, "Does Blues Man break knees or knuckles?"

Jason froze, becoming instantly awake. "What?"

"What does your cousin really do?"

He sat up and stared at her. "Does it matter?"

She shrugged. "Not really," she said, stroking the inside of his thigh. "I'm just curious."

He covered her hand and stopped her. She wanted to

distract him, and it was working. "He does a lot of things that you don't want to know about."

"It doesn't change anything. I still like him." She pressed her lips against his. "And I still like you."

Jason felt some of his tension dissipate. She accepted his cousin. That was a good sign. Maybe she would accept something else. "Are you free next weekend?"

"Yes, why?"

"I invited your sister and her husband over for dinner."

Abby sat up and stared at him, furious. "What? Why?"

He held his arms open, surprised by her anger. "I thought it was a good idea."

"But it's not."

"Why not? I wanted to give her a chance to get to know me. You didn't want me to talk to her in the office, so I thought this was the next best thing."

Abby briefly covered her face. "I can't believe you're doing this to me."

"What's wrong with having dinner with her?"

"Not here." Abby jumped out of bed and started to change. "Why didn't you tell me?"

"I'm telling you now."

"But not before you asked her."

He grabbed the hem of her shirt and pulled her down on the bed. "I'm sorry." He wrapped his arm around her waist and pressed her back against his chest, wishing she were naked, too. "I thought you'd be pleased."

She kept her back to him. "I'm not."

"I can tell."

She pulled at his arm. "Let me go."

"I don't want you to leave."

"I just have to go to the bathroom."

He sighed, then released her and watched her disappear into the other room.

* * *

Abby closed the bathroom door and silently screamed. Why did he have to ask Judith here? She knew he was trying to be kind, but she didn't want her sister at his place. Jason's place was the one space her sister couldn't have. Her sister had followed her everywhere. She didn't want her to follow her here. Not yet, at least. Not until she was more certain about her relationship with Jason. She didn't want her sister to be a part of this side of her life. She wanted Jason and his luxury apartment to herself. Judith already had it all, as their parents' favorite and the married one with a happy family and successful career.

Abby sat on the toilet, grabbed one of Jason's hand towels hanging on the wall and covered her face. She paused and sniffed it. Damn, even his towels smelled good. Every day she loved him more and more. She sighed. She was being selfish, but she didn't care. She'd already endured a holiday dinner with her sister and her perfect family. She didn't want to sit with Judith and her husband as they talked about their family and her sister dropping hints about Charles and Abby's failed relationship. She didn't want to listen to her sister tell Jason stories about what they were like growing up. She didn't want Jason to know too much about her past, not yet. At least not Judith's version. She needed more time.

Jason knocked gently on the door. "Abby, I'm sorry. I'll cancel if you want me to."

Abby hung up the towel and opened the door, full of hope. "Really?"

"Yes, we can have dinner with them another time."

"Next time let me organize it."

"Definitely."

"I know it sounds strange to you, but just trust me.

We'll have dinner with them, but we'll go to a restaurant. It can't be here."

"Whatever you say."

She grinned. "You're just being agreeable because you don't want me to leave."

He nodded. "Yes, that and I don't want you leaving with my shirt."

Abby glanced down and noticed that she'd put on his shirt instead of hers. In her anger, she hadn't even noticed that it didn't fit. It hung below her knees, and the sleeves covered her hands. She laughed. "Oh."

He unbuttoned it. "I like it. Even though my cousin compared me to a leprechaun."

Abby let the shirt fall to the ground. "Well, he's right. Because you're certainly getting lucky tonight."

A week later, Abby told Rosemary and Henry about meeting Jason's cousin while they cheered the success of Southern Taste. They'd invited her over to treat her. Jason hadn't been able to attend, but it had been a good meal. Abby felt relaxed as she helped Henry take one of the garbage cans out back.

"I wish Jason had been here. He should know all that you've done for us."

"You can tell him another time. I don't want him to get jealous and think I'm not thinking about his business enough."

Henry began to respond to her teasing, then paused when he heard a sound from behind them.

"Abby, go back inside," he said, pushing her toward the door.

"No, the lady should stay right there," a dark voice said.

Abby turned and saw two large figures dressed in all black appear out of the darkness.

Chapter 20

"Come on, you guys," Henry said. "Not here. Not now. Not with this nice lady around." One of the men stepped forward and knocked him to the ground.

Abby held out her purse and car keys. "Here's my purse, and you can have my car keys if you want."

One of the men moved forward and pushed her up against the building. "That's not what we're here for."

She pushed back. "This is all I have. What more do you want?" If they weren't after money or her car, Abby could only think of one other thing they wanted. She reached into her purse for her mace can, but the man saw the motion and seized her neck, squeezing tight enough that for a moment she couldn't breathe before he released her.

"I'm here to teach you a lesson. Stop snooping around."

"I'm not—"

He hit her hard across the face, then pointed at her. "I'm not done. This is the only time I'll say this. You and Ward had better stay away. Or we won't be this polite next time. You make sure Ward understands that." He hit her again, then two more times, until she tasted blood. When he lifted his hand to strike her again, she swung at the man, hitting him hard in the face with her bag. It stunned him just enough to loosen his grip.

"Run, Abby," Henry called out, still prone on the ground. The larger of the two men lunged at her, and she felt a sharp prick in her side before she took off, with the two of them pursuing close behind. She jumped over one of the railings and ran into the parking garage across the street from the restaurant. It was dimly lit and provided an excellent place for her to hide.

"Where is she?" she heard one of them say.

"Doesn't matter. I think we scared her pretty good. We can tell him he doesn't have to worry anymore." The man paused. "What the hell is that? You stabbed her?"

"She hit me."

The first man swore. "Get rid of it. If the bitch dies, it's on you."

Once she knew they were gone, Abby came out from where she was hiding behind one of the large commercial Dumpsters, and made her way back to Southern Taste. She stumbled to the back door of the restaurant, hoping that Henry was okay. When he opened the door, she felt a wave of relief.

Henry looked at her with horror, and she could hear footsteps coming down the alley. She turned to Henry to say something, but any words died on her lips when she saw him looking at her side. She followed his gaze and looked down, seeing blood creating a big dark stain on her blouse. She lifted the edge of her blouse and looked at the jagged gash that marred her skin. "Don't tell Jason," she managed to whisper; then everything went black.

"She's lucky. She's resting and will make a full recovery," the doctor told Henry and Rosemary as they sat in the waiting room. Once the doctor left, Henry buried his head in his hands, then cried out when his wife hit him.

He glared at her. "What was that for?"

"What have you gotten yourself involved in?"

"Nothing."

"Two times now we've had someone hurt in the alley when you go outside. That's not a coincidence. And why didn't you want to call the police?"

Henry shook his head, and his eyes filled with tears. "It was paid off. I don't know why they came back."

"What was paid off? Who came back?"

"I don't know. I just…I made a mistake. Just once, and Jason helped me."

"What kind of mistake?"

Henry let his shoulders fall, then told his wife the whole story about how he'd borrowed money to help save the restaurant.

"Who did you take a loan from?"

"Blues Man. But with the restaurant now doing well and the loan paid off, I didn't expect any more trouble."

"My God…if Jason finds out about this…"

Henry grabbed his wife's arm, his eyes pleading with her. "Please, don't say anything. Even Abby asked me not to."

"Why not?"

"Because he'll kill me. You know how he is. She was there when he got hurt. He won't understand this happening a second time. He'll blame me. He'll think this happened because of something I've done. Oh, God, I don't know what I'm going to do. And if he sees her like this… it will be too much like when you told me Gwen died. I promise you I haven't done anything to make them come back. I've never seen those guys before."

"We can't keep this a secret from him forever."

"I know. I just need some time while I try to figure this out."

"I think I know someone who can help us."

Beatrice sat at the side of Abby's hospital bed holding her hand, and cried. For a moment, her memory flashed back to years ago, when another young woman, a victim of a war she'd had no part of, lay in a similar bed, just like Abby, never to open her eyes again.

Thankfully Abby had opened her eyes, although briefly, and they lit up, though she couldn't smile. She reached out and squeezed Beatrice's hand.

"Do you have someone you want me to call?" Beatrice asked, taking Abby's hand in both of hers. "Your mother, or someone else?"

Abby shook her head, and tears streamed down her face. "Just you."

She'd said the words so slowly and deliberately, with an emphasis on "you," that Beatrice thought her heart would burst. As she looked at her now, calmly sleeping, Beatrice wondered how long she could keep what happened a secret from her son.

Jason looked at the text Abby had sent him and frowned. Unexpected trip. Will talk when I get back.

Why had she texted him and not called? How long was she going to be gone on her trip? Why hadn't she even told him where she was going? Was she getting back at him for going off the radar after the incident at the Madison Ball? He'd give her a few days' leeway, but no more than that. He told Henry just that when he visited Southern Taste for lunch. "What should I do when she gets back?"

"Who?"

"Abby. She sent me a strange text. I just told you ."

"Right, right." Henry tried to keep himself busy, although there really wasn't much for him to do. With the business thriving and their customer load practically full all the time, they had been able to hire additional staff so he didn't have to work on the floor most of the time.

Jason narrowed his gaze. "You're acting jumpy. Is something wrong?"

"No. I mean, why would anything be wrong?"

"Did she tell you something?"

"No." Rosemary called him from the back. "Sorry, gotta run," he said, then hurried away, and Jason watched him with growing suspicions.

Chapter 21

"Where is she?"

Henry jumped up from behind his desk and gaped at Jason, who stood like a raging warrior in the doorway. The restaurant had become a sanctuary to him, but now he felt like a caged animal. He swallowed hard. "Who?"

"Is she at home?" Jason said, making it obvious he wasn't in the mood to clarify.

Henry knew better than to pretend he didn't know what Jason was talking about, so he stood mute.

Rosemary rushed up behind him. "Keep your voice down, or the other patrons will hear you."

Jason kept his gaze focused on Henry. "Where is she?"

Henry's mouth went dry, and he looked to his wife for guidance.

Rosemary lightly touched Jason's sleeve with nervous fingers. "Jason, calm down. I don't know what you've heard, but—"

He spun to her, his eyes flashing. "Don't tell me everything is fine. I'll deal with both of you later," he said in an ominous tone. "Right now you have three seconds to tell me where Abby is."

"She's resting at home," Henry said.

"And she's not up to seeing anyone," Rosemary added.

Jason pushed past her. "Too bad, because she's going to see me."

Jason hardly remembered the drive to Abby's place. She'd lied to him. Abby wasn't out of town. She wasn't on some unexpected business trip. She had gotten hurt, and she'd kept it from him. He wasn't going to be angry, Jason told himself as he marched to her front door. He'd let her explain and he'd listen—at least try to—and he wouldn't get angry. He'd find out what happened and then deal with whatever needed to be done once he had all the information. He knocked on the door. When his mother opened it, he stood frozen for a moment, then his temper snapped. He swore. "She called you? She gets hurt, and she calls you?"

Beatrice yanked him inside. "Do you want the whole community knowing her business?" She closed the door. "Keep your voice down."

He saw Benny standing awkwardly in the background. He looked as if he didn't know whether to flee or hide.

Jason swore again. "And you knew about this, too?"

"Abby knew you'd get upset," Beatrice said.

He took a deep, steadying breath. "How bad is she?"

"She's getting better."

He firmly pushed his mother out of the way and headed to Abby's bedroom. "That wasn't my question."

Beatrice moved in front of him and blocked his path. "You've got to calm down first. This is the kind of behavior she was afraid of."

"Afraid of? You're saying she's afraid of me?"

"No, that's not what I meant."

He folded his arms. "When were you going to tell me?"

"I've been worried."

"And you think I wouldn't be?" He maneuvered past

her and grabbed the doorknob. Benny came up beside him and grabbed his sleeve. Jason shook his head and said in a low voice, "You don't want to do that."

He quickly let go. "We're thinking of Abby," Benny said. "You've got to calm down. She's already been through enough, and we don't want you to upset her."

"What about me? You all betrayed me."

"Jason, we just didn't want you to overreact," Beatrice said. "She begged us not to tell you, and I couldn't say no."

He turned away from them and swung the door open. When he saw her, the sound that escaped from his throat was the combination of a roar and a cry of anguish. He didn't know what he'd expected to see, but it wasn't this. His gaze swept over her bruised face, one eye swollen shut. He stumbled over to the bed, then fell to his knees, wanting to hold her but not wanting to hurt her, misery searing his heart. "I'll kill them all. I swear to you. I'll find them and kill them all."

Beatrice came up behind him. "Then you'll be put away for life."

"I don't care."

"Jason?" Abby said in a weak voice, reaching her free hand out to him.

He scrambled to hold her hand and grabbed it tight. "Yes, I'm here," he said, trying to sound as gentle as he could, although rage roiled inside him. "Tell me who did this to you."

"Don't be angry."

"I'm not angry with you," he said, kissing her hand, then pressing it close to his chest.

"I'm okay. I look worse than I am. It will be a while before I can help you—"

"Don't worry about me. Just get better." He sat on the

side of the bed. "Now, I want you to take your time and tell me what happened. Who did this?"

"I don't want you to get into any more fights."

"Abby," he said in low warning.

"Jason, don't tire her out," Beatrice said.

He sent his mother a threatening look—like that of a beast guarding its mate—and she withered under his gaze, stumbled backward, and immediately left the room. He turned back to Abby and lightly brushed hair from her forehead. "I'm not going anywhere. Just tell me what happened."

"How did you find out?"

"I'm not going to ask you again. Start talking."

"I was helping Henry take out some trash at the back of the restaurant when these two men showed up."

"The same as before?"

"No, different ones. Henry didn't seem to know who they were, and he was surprised to see them. They hit him. But then…" She paused for a moment, trying to gather her strength. "Then one warned me to stop snooping and that he was teaching me a lesson. It didn't make any sense. I don't know why it happened. I surprised one of them and hit him with my purse. When he let me go, I ran. I don't remember much of the rest." She paused again. "But it wasn't Henry's fault. I do remember him saying he's all paid up, and it wasn't like the usual shakedown."

"That's okay, you don't have to worry." He let her hand go and rested it on the bed. "You should have told me."

"They're dangerous men. I didn't want you to get involved."

"I am involved."

"But look at all that we've done. I don't want the progress we've made to be undone just because—"

"I can't leave this alone. You know me better than that. You want to protect me, but I have to protect you. I'll only promise one thing. That I won't kill them."

"Your mother told me about Gwen. How you'd both been caught in an unexpected turf war, and that was the reason she was killed."

"Yes, and I never got a chance to avenge her. I won't let that happen this time."

Abby struggled to sit up and winced.

"Where else are you hurt?" he asked, his tone sharp.

"Everywhere, but—"

"Did they kick you?"

"Jason." She sighed. "I got cut."

For a moment he couldn't breathe. "Are you telling me they stabbed you?"

"It wasn't deep. We can now say we have matching scars."

"That's not funny."

She stretched out her hand. "Forgive me."

He felt some of his anger ebb, and took her hand in his. "I will punish whoever is behind this, no matter what the price."

"I'm scared," Abby said in a small voice.

"Don't be. I'll protect you."

"No, I'm scared for you."

"I need you to trust me."

"I do—"

"Then don't *ever* keep something like this from me again." This time he couldn't keep from sounding angry. They had used a weapon.

"I hope something like this never happens again."

Jason pulled up the blanket to cover her, then stood, and when he spoke, his words had the resonance of a vow. "I plan to make sure it never does."

* * *

He hadn't kept her safe. It was Gwen and a spray of deadly bullets all over again. Damn it. The ugliness of his old world still came to haunt him. When Abby recovered, would she still want to be with him? Would this incident come between them forever? With her ex, she'd never had to be this afraid. He knew the fear he had seen in her eyes would haunt him more than the scars on her face and body. Being with him had threatened not only her livelihood, but her life.

He had to let her go. He couldn't protect her the way he wanted to. She deserved more, and he'd rather let her go than see her taken from him.

Chapter 22

He knew he'd come back for him. He didn't know when, he didn't know where, he just knew that Jason would come back for him, and it wouldn't be good. Not that anything had been good lately. Rosemary had kicked him out of the house, citing his betrayal as only one reason she didn't want to stay married to him. She kept him on at the restaurant because she still needed him, but she barely spoke to him. No matter how many times he told her that he didn't know why Abby got hurt, she shut him down.

"This isn't just about Abby. This is about you going to the Blues Man behind my back, lying to me about why Jason got injured, lying to me about how well the restaurant was doing."

"But I told you the truth."

"When it was almost too late."

"I just wanted to take care of everything for you."

"You're nothing but trouble."

He was now sleeping on his son's couch. He knew he couldn't stay there too long and would have to look for a place. But he didn't want to. He loved Rosemary and the life they'd built together. But she didn't believe him about that night, and he doubted he could get Jason to believe him either.

Henry's reckoning day was a warm April afternoon after the lunch crowd had gone. He was closing the trunk of his car, off to run an errand, when he heard a familiar, chilling voice behind him, and felt his blood turn cold.

"You lied to me."

He slowly turned and faced Jason. "I'm sorry."

"And you put Abby's life in danger."

"I don't know what happened. Truly. After you paid off that debt, I haven't borrowed a cent."

"Then why did they come here? Did they just want to chat?"

"I don't know," Henry said, throwing up his hands in frustration. "But they seemed to be more interested in Abby than me."

"If you're lying to me again…"

Henry waved his hands as if trying to brush the thought away, then rested a hand on his chest. "I swear I'm not lying. They weren't the same men. I've never seen them before."

"Why didn't you call me?"

Henry turned his head and rubbed the back of his neck, knowing he didn't have a good reply.

"Why?" Jason demanded.

"I didn't think you'd listen."

Jason swore. "Nobody seems to trust me anymore. And now I can't trust them."

"That's not it. Abby was afraid that you'd go looking for revenge."

"You're lying to me again. You didn't tell me because of Abby. You were afraid of what I'd do to you. You're a man, and you know how important it is to protect the ones you care for. Don't tell me that if Rosemary had been attacked, you'd be okay with me lying to you and telling you that she went on a holiday."

Henry sighed, ashamed. "I admit it. I'm not a man to be proud of," he said, his voice choked with tears. "I used Abby as an excuse not to tell you. I used Abby to get you to a hospital so that Rosemary wouldn't find out about the first shakedown. I seem to ruin everything I touch. Finally, for the first time in my life, I thought I was going to have a good life, and now it's all over."

Jason folded his arms and sent Henry a withering stare. "What the hell was that? Do you expect me to give you tissues? Do you expect me to feel sorry for you? To forgive you and say it's okay because life's been hard? I helped you. I got you out of trouble, and this is how you repay me?" Jason rested his hands on his hips. "Give me one good reason why I shouldn't punch you right now."

"I don't have one."

Jason grabbed Henry by his collar and shoved him up against the car. "Stop feeling sorry for yourself and think. And if you let one tear fall, I will belt you because you're crying for yourself and no one else. Now I'm going to say this slowly." He released his grip and smoothed out Henry's collar. "Give me one good reason why I shouldn't punch you right now. Think hard before you answer."

Henry chewed his lower lip and searched his mind for the right response. What did Jason want from him? What could he offer a man like him? He was a nobody. A man whose wife hated him, whose son now didn't respect him. But when he looked at Jason's hard gaze, he recognized that he was being given a second chance. Jason didn't have to listen to what he said; he had every reason to knock him down, but he hadn't. Henry felt his feelings of defeat slowly fade and a new resolve enter him. He'd spent his life being a weak man, but now Jason was giving him a chance to be strong. "I can help you."

Jason took a step back and nodded in a manner that said "I'm listening."

"I think Abby was targeted. They knocked me down, then they just went after her. Something's not right about this. Those men were wild—at least, one of them was. Not our usual kind. They saw her as a threat, and I don't know why. But maybe her attack was a message to you. Everyone knows you're a couple. No one would make a move like that without expecting retaliation. Unless…"

"Unless?"

"Unless the person who hired them didn't know who he was dealing with and doesn't have control over them."

"Or they did exactly what he wanted them to."

"We can't be certain it's a he."

"True."

"Who have you made angry recently?" Henry asked, relieved that he was no longer the focus of Jason's rage.

Jason sniffed and shook his head. "A man like me always has enemies."

"I need your help." Jason held up his phone and showed his cousin the picture of Abby's battered face. He'd had his mother take the photograph while Abby had been sleeping. He still had trouble looking at it, although he knew that Abby looked much better now. "I need you to find the men who did this."

Blues Man looked at the picture and frowned. "Who is that?"

"It's Abby."

"What the…" He snatched the phone, then stared up at him. "How many?"

"Two."

He set the phone down, and asked with caution, "Was she…?"

"No." Jason changed the image, and put his phone away. "She's doesn't look like that now, but—"

"Someone has to pay."

"Exactly."

Blues Man shook his head. "What the hell happened?"

"That's what I'm trying to find out."

"Where was she?"

"Southern Taste."

Blues Man's tone and gaze turned hard. "Henry has been loaning from somebody else?"

"Relax, nobody's stealing your business. Henry said that the men were not there for him, but for her."

His cousin swore. "That means the message was for you."

Jason nodded. "And I want to send a reply. I just don't know who to send it to." His phone rang. "Excuse me." He looked at the number, then sighed.

"Abby?" his cousin guessed.

"Yes."

"Aren't you going to answer it?" he asked when Jason let the phone continue to ring.

Jason turned the sound off and put it away. "I can't talk to her right now."

"You think staying away will keep her safe?"

He shrugged.

"Does she know that? If she doesn't, you should at least tell her."

"She won't listen to me."

Blues Man sighed. He rubbed his chin. "You know, I can find out who those men are."

"Yes."

"And I have no problem killing the messengers."

"No, I want them alive."

"And the person who sent them?"

Jason gripped his hand into fists. "I want them all to myself."

Dennis wiped his forehead as he tried to enjoy the vast city view from his downtown condo. How could it have all gone so wrong? He'd asked those goons to just scare her off. He hadn't expected them to take it so far. That hadn't been part of the plan.

"We made our flight, but it didn't arrive on time," the dark voice on the phone had told him that night, using code in case anyone overheard.

"You missed the flight?"

"No, I said it didn't arrive on time."

"What went wrong?" Dennis's heart had started to race. He was prepared for bad news.

"L got a little crazy. He took a knife onboard. It delayed us."

"He stabbed her?"

The voice grew quiet, and Dennis knew he'd made a mistake. "I don't think it was deep. Nothing to worry about. Anyway, we made it, so the trip was a success."

A success? Dennis wasn't so sure. Abby wouldn't talk now, but Jason wouldn't let an attack on Abby go unanswered. He'd wanted to teach her a lesson. Both of them. He wanted them to know that they couldn't push him around. He kept seeing their smug faces everywhere. Lately, every paper he looked in, he saw news about Jason's new venture.

He'd just wanted them out of his life, and now Jason could track him down if he wasn't careful. He could put certain pieces together. He'd told the goons to get out of the state, so that should help. He could still be okay. He hadn't heard about any deaths that could be hers, and Jason couldn't trace what happened back to him. Jason wasn't one to think straight when he was angry. He had to count on that. He'd put him in prison once; he could do it again. At least Abby wouldn't talk now. He was safe. That was what mattered. His business and the people who depended on him were safe from his past.

But no matter how much he told himself that story, Dennis felt a fissure of worry. Jason was more calculating and patient. Abby wasn't Gwen. Gwen had been so sweet, a girl he'd wanted for himself until Jason came along and took her away from him. Then bullets had taken her away from both of them.

He'd thought that money and women would have healed that wound, but it seemed to reopen every time, and seeing Jason moving on and happy while Dennis's business was struggling goaded him. He wanted Jason to suffer, too. He wanted him to always be reminded that he was from the gutter. That it was only because of him that Jason had made it as far as he had. That he was really a nobody. That was what had galled him. Gwen had fallen for a nobody. A guy with only five shirts that he washed until they were threadbare, but he still walked with pride. He'd survived the gang-infested streets and the lure of making easy money.

Even his own parents had been impressed with Jason when they fostered him. As if, because Dennis had been born middle class, he didn't have it as rough. He'd been called names for being too smart and not cool enough. He'd been shoved in lockers, and the girls hadn't looked at him because he wasn't a jock or on the student council.

Jason wouldn't even have met Gwen if it hadn't been for him. They hadn't gone to the same school. It was only because he'd had Gwen over to help her study, and Jason had come over to help his father clear up the backyard. The two of them had taken one look at each other and made him invisible. Again. Or rather, Jason had. He couldn't blame her. Girls always fell for guys like Jason. She hadn't known that; she'd just felt sorry for him. It was no more than that. But if she'd lived, he imagined she would have felt more.

Now Jason had a woman just like her. Someone far better than he deserved. Someone with beauty, class and grace. Someone who was trying to unearth Dennis's secrets so that Jason could take back the company. He'd just wanted to scare her away. Why had it gone so wrong?

Chapter 23

He was going to leave her. Abby could sense it and feared it, and she didn't know how to hold on to him. Her sister's words kept repeating in her mind. *He's just using you, and once he's through, he'll toss you aside the way...*

She hadn't seen her sister in weeks, giving her the excuse that she was traveling, and Judith had taken it at face value. She didn't want her family to know about the attack and judge Jason or Henry or anyone she'd come to care about. It had been nice to be pampered and spoiled by Beatrice and Rosemary. Jason had spared no expense for her care, offering to fly her anywhere she wanted, but she felt safe at home and wanted to be close to him, even if it meant only being in the same city. He'd come to check on her. Brief, sweet moments that always left her wanting more. He cared for her, worried about her and wanted to protect her, but that didn't mean he loved her.

She knew she couldn't make him love her, but she wanted to show him that he still needed her. She didn't know how, because the truth was he didn't. He could do business without her. He had the contacts he needed. She couldn't be a showpiece right now. Her face would heal, but would it heal fast enough before Jason found someone else? She pulled out her laptop and started putting together an idea—several—that she hoped would interest him. She didn't want him solely focused on finding the men who'd attacked her. If they wanted to have a future together, they couldn't just dwell on the past. Several hours had gone by when she heard the doorbell. Blurry-eyed, she answered it and saw Rosemary and Beatrice carrying two large bags.

"What a wonderful surprise," Abby said, welcoming them in. "Mmm…it smells delicious, but you don't have to keep doing this."

"I'm determined to add some more meat to those bones of yours," Rosemary said, heading for the kitchen.

The two women stopped when they saw Abby's dining table piled with papers and her laptop on.

"You should be resting," Beatrice said.

"Thanks to you, I'm much better now. I'm thinking of returning to the office next week. I have another idea that I think Jason will like."

"He'll like you to get better."

Abby sighed. "He won't even answer my calls."

"He gets this way when he's preoccupied."

It wasn't like him to not talk to her this long. It wasn't like the time when he disappeared. She'd felt a wall build between them during the time since she'd last seen him. "I know he really will like this idea," she said, going to her laptop.

Beatrice grabbed her arm and led her to the couch. "Sit down."

She did. "If you want to eat, I can clear the table."

Beatrice held her hand. "Abby."

"I have to think of business. It can't stop just because of a little—"

"It's going to be okay."

Tears filled her eyes. "No, it won't, and you know it, too. He's not talking to me or to you, just like in the beginning. He's shutting us out."

Rosemary came in and flopped into the chair in front of them. "Men make us miserable. We're better off without them."

"You're not helping."

She shrugged. "I love Jason, but what he's doing is wrong. He should at least talk to her. I wonder if Henry learned to lie from him."

"Why don't you just admit that you miss him?" Beatrice asked.

"Miss him? Do you know how much trouble he's caused me?" Rosemary replied.

"And did he apologize?" Abby asked.

"Many times, but—"

"Give him a second chance. I'm only saying that because I know you want to." Beatrice said.

"I want him to suffer."

"While you suffer, too?"

"At least you know he loves you," Abby said.

Rosemary and Beatrice shared a look. "Jason loves you in his own way," Beatrice said softly.

"I want to believe you, but I can't, not yet. He just needs to know that I'm okay and that I can help him. That's the only language he understands."

But Abby doubted her new strategy when she finally met Jason a week later. To her delight, he had responded to her phone call and agreed to see her at his place, but as she told him about her ideas, she could tell he wasn't paying attention. She sensed that all his answers were merely indulgent. She didn't want to be clingy; she knew he hated that. But she wondered if he was spending time with someone else. She used to know every aspect of his schedule, but now there were big holes in it. Even Benny kept her in the dark. She would fight for him.

"Let's talk about something else," she said, then she kissed him, spicing it up by darting her tongue in his mouth before pulling away. She saw his eyes darken, and knew she'd caught his interest. Soon she was naked in his arms.

It had been so long since she'd had him all to herself like this. So attentive and sexy. She'd expected it to feel routine, but being the magician he was, her body seemed to tingle at his every touch. She loved the smell of his skin, the hardness of his body, and he filled her with a pleasure that made her senses spin. After they drew apart, he gathered her close, and Abby felt tears in her eyes. Was this how Charles was able to deceive her? She'd made love to her ex-husband many times, not knowing about the other woman on the side. The one he truly loved. Was she just a basic routine? But the difference she was feeling wasn't about Charles; it was about her. The love she felt for Jason had seeped into the core of her being.

With Charles, she'd been willing to forgive him, but she felt more selfish now. She didn't want to share. They had nothing formal between them. Even if they had, she wouldn't be able to turn a blind eye. Jason had a lot more temptations than Charles had. Would she be able to keep him faithful?

When she heard Jason finally fall asleep, Abby slipped out of his grasp and left the room. She stood on the balcony, thinking of the opulence and riches surrounding her. Was she really ready to give up all this? Was there a price to pay for being with a powerful man who could get whatever and whoever he wanted? She wanted to fight, but if someone else held Jason's heart, Abby knew she'd already lost. The pain of that hit her, and hot tears fell down her cheeks, sobs wracking her body.

"Hey, what's wrong?"

She shook her head, embarrassed. She didn't want his pity.

He tenderly turned her to face him. "What's going on?"

She kept her head lowered, wiping her eyes. "If you don't like the idea—"

"The idea is great," Jason said, confused. "You know that. When you're better—"

She lightly touched his hand, relieved when he didn't pull away. She hadn't been able to touch him like this in days. "I'm better now and ready to work. I'll do a lot of the behind-the-scenes stuff."

He sighed. "Abby."

She held up her hand and shook her head. "Don't say it."

"What?"

She let her hand fall. "Don't say I need to rest or that I need time to heal. What happened was awful, but my mind still works." She clasped her hands together to keep them from shaking. "So, have you heard anything?"

"Nothing concrete yet."

"Let me help you."

"No," he said in a flat tone.

"I can't just sit on the sidelines. We make a good team. What have you been doing? Where have you been looking? I bet you've gone to Blues Man, right? What does he have to say?"

Jason glanced out at the horizon and sighed.

"What?"

He shifted his gaze to her face. "It's not going to work."

Dread crawled up her skin. It was too soon for him to say words like that. She walked back into the bedroom.

"It will." She sat on the bed and looked up at him. "I won't be able to attend the—"

His gaze flashed with annoyance. "You know I'm not talking about you attending anything with me. I don't need you to be my business partner."

"But that's what I'm good at. Please, don't throw me away because—because of a few scars. They'll heal. The doctors says I'll be as good as new."

"Throw you away?" His voice cracked. "Listen, there are things in my past that I don't want you exposed to."

"It's too late now."

"It's not too late." He sat on the bed beside her. "Until I figure out what happened, it's better if we don't see each other. Safer."

"Why?" She shook her head in frustration. "Nothing will happen to me."

"It already has."

"I mean, you don't need to keep me safe by pushing me aside. What happened that night wasn't your fault."

He leaned forward and lowered his voice, the heat of anger darkening his eyes. "Yes it was, and I'm going to figure out why."

"And when you do?"

He glanced away.

Abby jumped to her feet. "Why don't you just admit it? You don't need me anymore. That's why you don't want to see me. You don't care if the scars heal. You've already moved on."

"You're still beautiful, and your scars are almost gone," he said, his voice filled with rage.

"Then why are you pushing me away?"

"I just told you."

"You're lying. You're using it as an excuse, but you don't have to." She glared at him. "I really thought you were different, but I was wrong. You only came to me for one reason, and I got that for you. The rest was just extra—icing on a cake. Fine. I understand. But don't try to be noble. Don't pretend that you really care and that's why you're letting me go, because if I really mattered, you'd fight to stay together."

Jason seized her shoulders. "Listen, Gwen—"

Abby eyes widened. "What?"

He swore.

"Did you just call me Gwen?"

"No, I was going to tell you that Gwen—"

Abby shook her head and pushed him away. "I don't care. I don't want to know. Before I did, but you're right. She was the woman you loved, and she died. But the truth is she didn't. She haunts you. She haunts every decision you make."

"That's not true."

Abby grabbed her clothes.

Jason pulled her roughly to him and buried his face in her neck. "Please, believe me, Abby," he said, his words deep with emotion. "Forgive me. You've made me the happiest I've been since—"

"Gwen?" she said bitterly.

"No, my entire life. I've seen a lot of ugliness in my life. Gwen never did. She'd had a charmed life until…" He let his words die away. "You make me forget things. You keep seeing me as a better man than I really am. I want to live in the future, but I have a past that won't leave me alone, and I don't want to ever see you hurt again. I don't want to let you go, but if it will keep you safe, I will."

For a moment she thought she heard tears in his voice. She steeled herself against them, raw grief engulfing her. Because she wanted him to know that this was a fight they could battle together. That he didn't have to be a lone warrior anymore. She wanted to hold him as close as he held her, but she stubbornly kept her arms by her side. If he really cared, he wouldn't let her go. He'd act as if they were one. She squeezed her eyes shut, inhaled his scent and reveled in being in his arms one last time, before she swallowed and said in a cool tone, "Goodbye, Jason."

He didn't release her, and for one wild moment she feared he wouldn't and would break her resolve. Then he sighed, resigned, and let her go, looking at everything in the room except her. "Bye," he said, then walked away and out of her life.

Chapter 24

Abby didn't cry after Jason left. Instead, she decided to focus on work. Her sister had been right about Jason. Instead of working exclusively with him, she should have focused on building her clientele, and she would now. She'd gotten a few referrals from Rosemary and would follow up on them. The money she'd made from working with Jason would allow her to find another place. She couldn't take working with her sister anymore. She wanted to be away when Judith found out that her relationship with Jason was over. Her sister would send her looks of triumph. She could already imagine her words. "See? Didn't I tell you he'd dump you once he didn't need you anymore?" Her heart was already broken, and she wasn't in the mood to swallow another bitter pill. She'd show Judith, Jason and Charles that she didn't need anyone. That she'd learned her lesson.

"I'm off to get drinks with the girls," Judith said, rushing out the door. "Don't work too late."

Abby didn't look up from her monitor. She hated when her sister pretended to care. She groaned in annoyance when the phone rang. It was after hours, and she didn't expect any calls.

"Hello?"

"Hi, this is Stephen. Is Judith there?"

"No, she just left."

"Sorry for calling your phone. I just thought she may be in your office before going off to spend a night out with her girlfriends."

"No, she's not here." Abby paused. "Did you say *a night out*?"

"Yes."

Abby found his statement odd. Judith didn't spend a night out. She went shopping with her girlfriends or gambling, but spending a night out with them wasn't her sister's usual way of doing things. Abby spent another hour finishing making calls for one of her clients before getting ready to leave for the day. She checked the waiting area and noticed that Judith had forgotten to lock her office door. That wasn't her sister's way. Judith was very private. Even as children, she always kept her room locked.

Curious, Abby walked over and peeked in, and noticed something lying on the floor, off to the side. Abby crept inside, feeling as she had when she was younger and had stolen a pair of earrings from her sister's jewelry box, and picked it up. It was a napkin with the name the Atrium nightclub printed on it. A phone number was scrawled in bright red ink across it. What was her sister doing going to the Atrium? She knew she had a wild streak in her—so did she—but she was a married woman now. That club wasn't a place her husband would feel comfortable going to. Could that be where she had gone after work? But with whom?

Abby knew Judith would never go to a club like the Atrium with her girlfriends. Abby swore. No matter the consequences, she had to find out what her sister was up to. She looked at the number for the Atrium and dialed it. When someone picked up, she said, "I was wondering if you could tell me if you have a certain guest visiting with you this evening."

"I'm sorry ma'am," a polite voice said on the other side of the phone. "But it's our policy never to reveal the name of anyone visiting our establishment."

"I understand, but there's been an accident and I need to get a message to this person right away. I can't get her on her cell phone. I've tried three times."

"If you want to give me the message, I can have it passed on, if the individual you want to reach is visiting with us this evening."

"Oh, thank you so much. I need to get a message to a Ms. Judith Watson. Tell her that her husband Stephen has been trying to reach her. One of the kids got sick and had to be…" She stopped and hung up. Telling a lie like that was cruel. There had to be another way to uncover Judith's secret life. Abby looked down at the discarded napkin and dialed the number.

"Hello, Judith," a male voice said.

Abby's heart began to pound. Shoot, she'd forgotten about caller ID. At least she'd used her sister's business phone.

"Judith?"

Her mouth went dry. She knew that voice. It was one she'd never forget no matter how hard she tried.

"Hello?"

She hung up, her head spinning before everything began to come into focus. Why did Judith have a napkin from the Atrium with Dennis Collins's cell phone number? How long had they known each other? Was she the reason Dennis had found out about her and Jason going to the Madison Ball? No one else besides Judith knew they were going to the ball and had a direct connection to Dennis. She knew her sister had been annoyed that Jason had taken her shopping and bought her a dress and some other items. She remembered Judith even convincing poor Stephen to purchase a new necklace for her. But had Judith taken their competition to a new level?

Had Judith deliberately made sure that Dennis was at the Madison event to sabotage her? Had she wanted to win the bet that bad? What had she told him? What had made Dennis so belligerent toward her? Abby left her sister's office, determined to find out.

A hot, humid summer evening settled over the city that Friday night. At the Atrium, the ladies wore their very best. Abby didn't have to look through the smoke-clouded, dark room for long before she saw her sister sitting at the bar, cradling a glass of wine.

"So this is where you go to hang out with your girlfriends?" Abby asked, sliding into a seat next to her. She looked around. "Where are they, by the way?"

Judith stared at her, openmouthed.

Abby grinned. "Surprise!"

"What are you doing here?" she stammered.

"I think I'm the one who should be asking you that question."

Judith reached for her glass. "Please, don't start."

Abby moved it out of reach. "Stephen called the office after you left. He thinks you're out with your girlfriends."

"He doesn't know I like to come here."

Abby was quiet for a moment. "By yourself?"

"Yes, it's good to have a few secrets in a relationship. I know how to keep a marriage going, unlike some."

Abby picked up her sister's glass, determined not to be provoked. "Of course, you're the expert."

"Give me back my drink."

Abby kept it out of reach, setting it down hard enough that some of the liquid splashed over the side.

"Be careful," Judith snapped. "Do you know how much a drink here costs?"

"On a budget, are we?"

"Don't sound so superior. You won't have access to Jason's money for long."

"True. So, do the kids you have even belong to Stephen?"

"Of course they do!" Judith said, outraged. "I'm not having an affair!"

"Could have fooled me. I discovered that you've been coming here and meeting up with a certain someone."

"Now, what are you talking about? You're always accusing me of something. You don't know how much that hurts me."

"That's because you're always up to something."

"I don't know what you're talking about."

"Yes. You. Do." Abby shoved the shriveled up napkin in front of her. "I found this in your office. You're the one who told Dennis where Jason and I were that night."

"So?"

"Why?" Abby lifted the glass and held it over Judith's dress.

"What are you doing?"

Abby started to tilt the glass. "Tell me why."

"I didn't want you to win!"

Abby paused. "What did you tell him?"

"Nothing."

Abby tilted the glass again, knowing her sister would prefer her husband finding out about her nighttime activities over having a designer dress ruined. "You'd better tell me the truth."

"Okay, okay," Judith said with a note of panic. "Please, put the glass down."

Abby didn't move. "Start talking first."

"I just implied that you and Jason had some goods on him, that you planned to use that night to embarrass him and that Jason was planning to try to get the business back. I just wanted him to show up and make a scene. I couldn't stand the thought of you winning. You and Jason were so happy together, and it was annoying. And I shouldn't have made the bet in the first place because I knew I couldn't afford to pay up, so I had to do something."

Abby stared at her sister for a long moment, unable to recognize her. She knew her sister could be a snake. She knew that she could lie, and that at times she could be competitive, but she'd never realized how selfish she could be.

"You could have told me." But as she said the words, she already knew the answer. Her sister had too much pride. At least she now knew the reason Dennis had warned her. Why he'd acted so paranoid. He had secrets, and her sister had made him think Abby and Jason knew what they were. For the first time, she really saw her sister. She now could imagine that she had broken the statue Jason had given her on purpose.

"You went too far, Judith."

"I know, and I'm sorry, but everything is all right now. Nothing really happened. And I'll make it up to you, I promise." Judith nervously licked her lips. "Now, please, put the glass down."

Abby stood, then slowly poured the glass on her sister's lap, a grin touching the corners of her mouth at the sound of her sister's screams.

An early fall sun tinted the trees in the distance with its golden rays. Beatrice studied the landscape, then let her gaze fall on her son. He stood on the balcony, even more despondent than he'd been after Gwen died. She remembered when he'd designed the mountain house to the dimensions he and Gwen had dreamed of. He needed to move on with his life. Get a house that suited him and his new life. She walked up and stood beside him.

"Abby's not coming," she said.

He watched a hawk soar through the sky. "I don't expect her to."

"Then how long are you going to sulk?"

"I'm not sulking." Jason rested his forearms on the railing.

"After pleading for forgiveness, Rosemary finally let Henry back in the house."

Jason nodded. "That's good."

"You could learn something from him. Keeping secrets isn't good for a relationship."

Jason rubbed the back of his neck, but nothing seemed to ebb the tension there. "I'm not keeping anything important from Abby."

"You know I won't always be here for you."

"You're not going anywhere," he said in a sharp tone. "The chemo's over, and the doctor says you're in remission."

Beatrice sighed. "It doesn't have to be this way. Tell her the truth."

"I don't care what she thinks of me as long as she's safe."

She hit him hard on the back of the leg.

He swore and stared at her, stunned, rubbing the spot where she had hit him. "Mom!"

"Yes, exactly, I'm your mother and I want you to listen. Stop being an idiot."

"An idiot?"

"You're hurting both of you because you're scared."

"And so was Gwen! She was afraid that night when she came to the apartment, but I told her she'd be fine. Even her parents had been leery. We always met at her place, in her neighborhood, but I wanted to spend time with her so I told her to come. I wanted her to have your signature chicken soup with dumplings and—"

"And we had a great time," Beatrice cut in.

"Until I put her in the car to take her home," he said in a grave voice.

"You wouldn't have known. You did nothing wrong."

"I fell for the wrong girl."

"You think if she'd grown up in the same neighborhood, she would have been safer?"

"She would have been used to it." He shook his head. "I know it doesn't make sense."

"Exactly, because your fear is irrational. Abby is a fighter. She's strong, and it's better to have happy moments together, no matter how long or short they may be. Don't do this."

"She'll forget me. Let her anger protect her. It's a price I'm willing to pay."

"You're not trying to protect Abby. You're protecting yourself. You're afraid to love."

Jason gripped the railing, his voice raw with emotion. "I can't love like that again."

"When are you going to admit that you already do?"

His cell phone rang. A look of relief crossed his face before he glanced at the number, then he answered. "Yes?" He nodded a few times, then said, "I'm there," before he hung up.

"Who was that?" Beatrice asked as Jason walked inside.

"Blues Man has some news."

Chapter 25

Jason sat across from his cousin, unable to process all that he'd heard. Dennis had been behind Abby's attack? "Okay." He leaped to his feet, ready to act.

"Sit down, cuz," Blues Man said in a neutral tone.

"Why?"

His tone hardened. "It's time we had a talk."

"About what?" Jason said, annoyed. "We can talk later."

"What you planning on doing, now that you know Dennis was behind your woman getting hurt?"

"You know what I have to do."

He shook his head. "No, I don't. I'm thinking you're planning on doing what you want to do, regardless of the consequences."

"What do you mean by that?"

"Well, as I see it, those two stooges gave him up pretty quickly. Too quickly. This was kid's stuff, but now that we know, I have the means to take care of him for you."

"You know I've got to do it myself."

"Why?" Blues Man asked, looking bored.

Jason stared at him, amazed. "What do you mean why? Because of Abby."

"No, you mean because of Gwen."

"This time around, I'm gonna take care of business myself."

"At that time it was an East Coast versus West Coast thing, and Gwen got caught in the war."

Jason gripped his hand into a fist. "Collateral damage."

"Something like that," Blues Man said in a detached tone.

"And those bastards went on killing until one of them was shot dead and the other guy ended up on death row after shooting a police officer."

"At the time, you couldn't have done anything about it."

"Yes, I could. I could have taken my own revenge."

"And ended up in prison, like so many of the brothers we grew up with on the street. Or I could be visiting your grave right now. Or maybe not. Cemeteries freak me out." Blues Man removed his sunglasses. He rarely did so, his eerily silver gaze making people more nervous than his shades. "Remember, man, it was your testimony that finally helped identify the trash who took your lady out."

"He had them stab Abby."

"I know, but let me take care of this."

"No, this is real personal to me. I have to do it myself."

"That's why we need to talk. Man, it's time for you to stop walking both sides of the track."

"I don't know what you mean."

"Yes, you do. You have everything now, and I don't want to see you throw it all away just because of your false sense of pride. Cuz, you left the hood a long time ago. I was jealous at first. You seemed to have left us behind, enjoying your high-class way of living, with your big house, fine wine and dining and all the perks that come with being part of the acknowledged establishment, while I struggled to gain my foothold in the streets with my off-line wheeling and dealing.

"We were both in business, but your momma saw you as successful, and kept telling me I needed to start going straight. Hell, at times I was making four times what you were, but she never saw me as having succeeded, still doesn't. But you, you had achieved her dream of being an upstanding businessman. Even though your reputation was rough, you made it work for you. People feared you, and that gave you power.

"When that thing happened to you several years ago and you went to prison, I was blown away. I couldn't believe it. I knew then that someone or somebody had manufactured some kind of false accusations against you. There was no way my squeaky clean cuz would be caught engaging in fraud. Do you know how much it pained me to see you destroyed like that?

"Then, you get out, and I hear you're getting your life back together. Before I know it, you go and start fighting again. I couldn't believe you were still doing that, but I was a little proud. Remember when I first tried to recruit you? I knew we'd work well together, but you turned me down flat because you wanted something more. So here's my question—do you still want that?"

"I have it."

Blues Man shook his head, sad. "No, you're slipping. You can't wear a suit and act like a thug and expect people to see you as a gentleman. It never works that way. One thing that works in my business is fear. That's how I retain my power, and that's how I get respect. That's the main currency in my business. It's not the same for you. It doesn't have to be. It's time you made a choice and stop trying to live both ways. You either hang up your gloves or work with me."

"With you?"

"Hey, if you'd chosen me instead of Dennis, you wouldn't have ended up in prison."

"I still want to get him."

"Let me get him for you. I hire people to take care of my trash. You left the streets a long time ago, and that's where your badass behavior needs to stay. Make a new life for yourself with Abby. Leave Dennis to me."

"Isn't that the coward's way out?"

"You're already being a coward."

Jason stared at him, stunned. "What?"

"Your mother told me about you and Abby."

Jason swore. "I don't believe this."

"If you're really over her, I'll take over where you left off."

"Stay away from her."

"Why? You prefer someone else to have her?"

"She's mine."

Blues Man smiled. "Prove it."

"I will."

"I still envy you, cuz. I live and breathe in the shadows. But you have a chance to live in the light."

Chapter 26

Former CEO of SENTEL, Inc. Dennis Collins still cannot be reached for comment after being removed by the board of directors and facing charges of embezzlement.

Jason looked at the news with little interest. He knew Dennis had gotten off easy. At least he hadn't gone missing; that was usually Blues Man's style. He'd tried to contact Abby to let her know she had nothing to fear, but he hadn't been able to reach her. Outside, a gentle December snow fell, reminding him of her catching snowflakes on her tongue. His heart twisted.

Someone knocked on his office door, so he changed the image on his laptop before he said, "Come in."

Abby entered and sat down.

Jason gripped the side of his chair to stop himself from jumping up and grabbing her. "Hello," he said, cautious, unable to read her cool facade.

"Hi."

"I've tried to call—"

"Have you heard about Dennis?"

"Yes."

"My sister was the reason he showed up at the Madison Ball. I won't bore you with the details. I just thought you should know."

"I don't think—"

"Your cousin told me that I don't have to worry about you anymore. He told me about Dennis and the two men and that everything's been, in his words, washed clean. He used a lot of analogies to trash pickup and stuff, but I got the gist of it."

Jason blinked. "You spoke to Blues Man?"

She giggled. "Yes, he's so sweet. Have I told you how much I like him?" She took a seat in front of his desk.

Jason gritted his teeth. "Yes. Now—"

"But that's not why I'm here."

He swore.

She frowned. "What?"

"Are you going to let me finish a sentence?"

"Not yet. I have something I want to say first." Abby pulled out a photo and then pushed it over to him.

"What's this?" Jason asked, looking down at a picture of an unprepossessing, chubby young teenager with acne, braces and glasses.

"I want to tell you about her. She was the older sister of a pretty popular younger sister. She was bullied and ignored, but she didn't mind. She had her friends and enjoyed volunteering at the hospital. Look at her real good, even though she's not much to look at. You wouldn't have noticed her, would you? You wouldn't have wanted to protect her like some fragile flower. No one did, so she learned to protect herself. But then in her senior year, her acne cleared, she grew several inches, and boys' heads started to turn. She was smart, and this guy she married saw what she didn't and used it. She felt grateful someone like him would even notice her."

Abby tapped her chest. "When I say I know how it feels to be misunderstood, I mean it. When I say I can take the pain, I mean it. You can look at me now and think that I've always had it easy, but I haven't. What happened scared me, but it also made me stronger because I've had to be. I've had to survive a painful divorce, starting over, and I'm not going to let you ruin what we have. I'm not some damsel that needs to be rescued. We make a good team. We can rescue each other."

He paused then asked, "Are you finished now?"

"Yes."

He waved the photograph. "This is an awful picture."

"I know."

"I've also seen it before."

Abby stared at him for a long moment, in disbelief, not sure she'd heard him correctly. She'd bared her heart to him, and he looked amused. Was he going to compare her awkward photo to some animal as other kids had? Call her an owl or giraffe? She knew she'd taken a risk coming to see him, but after talking to his cousin, her hope had been renewed. Now she felt it plummet. She stiffened in her seat. "Are you making fun of me?"

"No, I'm not. I've seen this picture before."

"What? How?"

"Your sister showed it to me once."

"My sister?" Abby said, feeling both anger and shock at the same time.

"Yes," Jason said with a note of mischief. "If you can talk to Blues Man behind my back, I can talk to your sister."

"And she showed you that picture?" Abby asked, pointing to the photo in horror.

He nodded. "She wanted to tell me that you weren't all

that you seemed. That if I wanted a real makeover, she knew someone who could help."

"I knew she was stealing clients from me," Abby said in a burst of anger.

"When I wouldn't fall for that angle, she told me how she's always been jealous of you."

"She said that?"

"Not in those exact words, but I could guess from the stories she told. She told me about you wearing some ugly sweater your grandmother knit for you, and of you being the date for your cousin's prom, even though he was a foot shorter than you. I think she thought telling me those stories would change my opinion of you, but she was wrong." His eyes captured hers. "What she told me only made me love you more."

Abby blinked, feeling suddenly light-headed. "Love me?"

"Yes. You were beautiful long before you knew it." He stood, walked around the desk, took her hands and lifted her to her feet. "So, can I keep this?"

Abby stared at him, confused. "No."

Jason wrapped her arms around him, a teasing grin touching his lips. "Why not?"

"Because it was hard enough to show you once."

"Want to make an exchange, then?"

"What will you give me?"

He reached behind him and opened a drawer, then set a small jewelry box on the table. "How about this? It's up to you to accept." When she didn't move, he frowned. "Aren't you going to open it?"

Abby shook her head.

"Why not?"

"You weren't supposed to do this."

"I rarely do what I'm supposed to."

"But I'm not prepared. You told me that you didn't want to see me anymore. That we should split up. I thought I'd have to convince you—"

He brushed his lips against her forehead, his breath warm against her skin. "You have. You've convinced me that my life isn't right without you. That you're strong enough to accept me as I am. And I'm strong enough to love you as much as I do," he said in a deep voice that echoed the feelings of his heart. "I was going to come by tonight, but you beat me to this moment." He held up the box, his gaze steady but unsure. "Please, open it."

Abby bit her lip, then took the small jewelry box and opened it. A large diamond ring sat inside. "It's beautiful," she said in awe. She took the ring out and put it on her finger. "I've never been given a promise ring before."

Jason swore. "A promise ring? I'm asking you to marry me."

Abby laughed, then threw her arms around his neck, her heart feeling as if it could float. "I know. I just wanted to hear you say the words."

A year later

Abby hummed along to the carols on the radio as she drove home under a dark blue sky. She'd hoped for snow, but knew there wouldn't be a white Christmas this year. However, she couldn't complain. Her business was booming, Jason was the head of SENTEL again, and his resorts were expanding. Her sister had chosen another line of work, and she looked forward to hosting her parents, Beatrice, Henry, Rosemary, Benny and Blues Man for a special holiday dinner tomorrow evening. But snow would have been nice.

Abby's thoughts of snow disappeared as she drove up

the long winding driveway and saw the mansion aglow with holiday lights. A large evergreen tree was exquisitely decorated with white lights, large silver blubs and golden streamers. Jason opened the front door and greeted her.

"So, what do you think?" he asked.

Abby stepped out of the car, stunned. "It's wonderful."

"I hired a team to make sure everything would look just the way you'd want it to. But I have another surprise for you. Close your eyes."

When she did, he took her hand and led her through a shortcut to the back of the house.

Abby followed him, wondering what his surprise could be, then she felt something light falling around her. She opened her eyes and stared up, amazed, as large snowflakes drifted about her, blanketing the ground in white. Abby slowly spun around, speechless, tears touching her eyes. With the help of an expert crew and a snow machine, Jason had created a winter wonderland, reminding her of the snow stories she'd told him about. He'd made her holiday wish come true.

"Let's build a snowman together," Jason said.

Abby bent down and picked up the snow, then shook her head, disappointed. "I'm sorry, but you ordered the wrong type of snow."

His face fell. "What? I did? Let me—"

Abby laughed, then threw her arms around him. "Just kidding." She kissed him, hoping he could taste the depth of her love for him. She was happy to share her life with him. "Everything is perfect."

Jason swore, wrapping his arms around her waist. "I knew you had a mean streak."

Abby caressed the side of his face, still in awe that this man was hers. The man she'd seen in a restaurant and had fantasized about. The man who'd stolen her heart and given her his own. "I still have to work on that filthy mouth of yours," she teased.

A slow, devilish smile spread on her husband's face. "You have the rest of my life to try."

* * * * *

REQUEST YOUR FREE BOOKS!

2 FREE NOVELS
PLUS 2 FREE GIFTS!

KIMANI™ ROMANCE

Love's ultimate destination!

There is no
turning back...

KPJMJ3841214